AF437173

TWO-TIMING TILLIE
Femme Fatale

Also by **ESMERALDA LINTNER**

THE GANJA NETWORK 2

THE ELEGANCE OF LIFE

GABRIELLE'S HEART
An Angel's Touch

FIFI'S EROTIC BOUTIQUE
A Store of Pleasure

LINCOLN MEETS WASHINGTON
An Historical Fantasy

FIFI'S NAUGHTY RHYMES and FAIRY TALES
Make Believe Erotica

FIF'S NAUGHTY RHYMES and FAIRY TALES
Volumes 2 and 3

TRUMP: THE PRINCE OF FOOLS
A Musical Fantasy

TEDDY, HARRY and DICK
The Presidents Speak

LADY FARTINGHAM
An Historical Tale in
Flatulent Taste

REVEREND STIFFWILLY
A Heavenly Endowment

TWO-TIMING TILLIE

Femme Fatale

by

ESMERALDA LINTNER

Copyright 2021 by Esmeralda Lintner

This book is a work of fiction.
References to real people, events, establishments,
organizations or locales are intended
only to provide a sense of authenticity
and are used fictitiously. All other characters,
incidents and dialogue are drawn from the author's
imagination and are not to be construed as real.

All rights reserved. This book may not be
reproduced in whole or in part without
written permission from the publisher in
any form except in the case of brief
passages used for review, nor may any
part of this book be reproduced, stored in a
retrieval system or transmitted in any
form or by electronic, mechanical,
photocopying, recording or other
means without written permission
from the publisher.

Cover design provided by kdp.amazon.com

Please see separate ACKNOWLEDGMENTS page
for information on song lyrics used in the text

ISBN 9798709460942
First printing May 2021

Printed in the United States of America

CONTENTS

ACKNOWLEDGMENTS

"I Wanna Be Loved By You"
Herbert Stothart, Harry Ruby, Bert Kalmar
"Ain't Misbehavin'"
Andre Razaf, Fats Waller, Harry Brooks
"You're the Cream in my Coffee" and
"It All Depends on You"
Ray Henderson, Buddy G. DeSylva, Lew Brown
"Ma! He's Making Eyes at Me"
Con Conrad, Sidney Clare
"Jumpin' Jive" (also known as **"Hep-hep!"**)
Cab Calloway, Frank Froeba, Jack Palmer
"Some of These Days"
Shelton Brooks
"My Blue Heaven"
Walter Donaldson, George A. Whiting
"Can't Help Lovin' Dat Man"
Jerome Kern, Oscar Hammerstein II
"Someone to Watch Over Me"
George & Ira Gershwin, Howard Dietz
"Bésame Mucho"
Consuelo Velázquez
(English lyrics: Sunny Skylar)
"Quizás quizás quizás" Osvaldo Farrés
(English lyrics: Joe Davis)

SLIM JIM'S PUNCTURED ROMANCE

On the south side of Chicago, tucked away from the maddening traffic and crowds, lies the *Pink Pussycat Club*. The regular customers who make their way in are always lively. They love to shake their tootsies on the dance floor, whirling away to the notes of a piano player perched on a slightly-risen stage. Right at the moment he's begun banging out the refrain from the popular hit, *Sweet and Lowdown*. He alternates such fast numbers with a ballad or two to give the dancers a little breather. Soon he breaks into his rendition of *That Certain Feeling*. The darkened cellar-like room is filled with cigarette smoke. Couples squeeze into chairs placed around small tables, drinking the now legally manufactured spirits thanks to the abolition of the Eighteenth Amendment. Their minds are still filled with scenes of uncorked barrels of beer swirling on barroom floors and the strains of people singing *Happy Days Are Here Again*. This night, however, is devoted to more serious pursuits: sipping cocktails, cuddling close and necking outright as the piano player continues his tunes nonstop.

After his final set before a well-deserved break, he steps off the raised stage. Lighting a cigarette of his own, he brushes a piece of pesky lint off his white suit coat and adjusts his black bowtie. He barely notices a line of chorus girls who emerge onto an adjacent stage. The curtain having gone up and signaling the house band to strike up a lively melody, the scantily-clad young women break into a goofy rendition of the latest dance craze, the Turkey Trot. The piano player crosses the narrow passage between the stage and the tables and finds a chair. Still drawing puffs on his cigarette, he straightens up and begins taking note of some of the more attractive chorines. Then he directs his attention to us as intruders upon his privacy.

"Oh, hello there," he says, "don't you just love them pretty dames? They're really shakin' them fannies tonight, I'll say! Naw, I don't mind ya botherin' me. I'm on my break anyway. My boss seems to think I've been on a break ever since I started workin' in this joint. But that's just his dumb old opinion."

He takes a long drag on the cigarette which is halfway burnt already, and the smoke emerges from his nose in two gray streams. "Y'know, I recall them early days when I started out in this biz. Oh, excuse my bad manners. I clean forgot to introduce myself. Slim Jim's the name --- at least that's what everybody's always called me. Somebody once told me I was the skinniest, toothpickenest piano player in town, can ya beat that? In spite of the fact that a good wind could blow this thin body of mine away, I sure as hell got my fill of the broads in them days. There's one particular gal I'll never be able to shake from my memory. She earned the name Two-Timing Tillie. She took me and a whole bunch other dumb clucks for a ride. She used me up and then left me high and dry. But oh, what a sexy babe she was! She could sing and dance, and she really stood out in the chorus line wherever she performed. That little minx had it all, I can tell ya that! What a toe-tapping flapper she turned out to be. She stole the show *and* my heart without even tryin'. There'll never be another like Tillie."

Snuffing out the now stubby cigarette in a nearby ashtray already full of other customers' discarded butts, Slim Jim continues, "I warn you men out there to be on your guard. A little vixen like her can always weave a web of lies and deceit, and you'll get caught right in it. Heaven help ya if you're plannin' to escape from her clutches. She'll have ya right where she wants, and you're as good as dead." Shaking his head, he chuckles and adds, "Believe it or not, though, I have fond memories of her still. Y'see, I used to be manager up at the glitzy *Diamond Rose Carousel*. That's when I lived in New York and could walk over from 43rd Street. The day I first laid eyes on that *femme fatale* is etched forever in my brain."

Slim Jim stares off beyond the crowded club and its patrons. He goes into a sort of half-awake half-asleep trance as he continues to reveal his story, thinking all the while to himself without speaking to us directly from here on out.

That night she stepped on to the stage was memorable, he reflects. Just looking at her grabbed my heart strings. I was acting as Master of Ceremonies that night. When she and the line of three other chorus girls came out, I announced them like this: "Ladies and Gentlemen, I have the honor and privilege of presenting for your entertainment our latest discovery. Let's give a nice round of applause for The Four Little Chicakadees!" As the polite clapping rang throughout the crowded club, I added, "They're gonna to perform that dance craze that has captured the nation and the world: the Charleston!"

The girls danced frantically, putting their entire souls into the performance. They brought much enjoyment to the club's patrons. The applause was deafening, and immediately they broke into their version of another popular dance craze, the Black Bottom. The crowd went berserk when the prettiest and most charming of the chorines stepped forward. That was Tillie. She turned out to be the glittering star of the night. The other "Little Chickadees" cleared the stage for her as she prepared for her big moment. I grabbed the house microphone and yelled over the hoots, hollers and shouts of approval, "Now let's watch this adorable little chickadee tap her way into our hearts. Get ready to swing the night away with Tillie!"

The band struck up the now familiar tune. In a screechy but quite acceptable voice, almost sultry, Tillie sang and danced to the lively rhythm:

I want to be loved by you, just you,
And nobody else but you,

I want to be loved by you, alo-o-ne!
Boop-boop-a-doop!

I want to kissed by you, just you,
Nobody else but you,
I want to be kissed by you, alone!

Her performance was good enough to razzle-dazzle the audience members. Her glittery presence was enhanced by the shaking and shimmying of her lithe body. That babe sure knew how to keep the onlookers' attention. She was wild, and the entire night took on a unique wildness, too.

There were times when some men were really puttin' it away, as the saying goes. As a result they became drunk and extremely rowdy. A few got so snockered that they began whistling like a wild pack o' wolves. One or two tried to grab at Tillie. Fortunately she knew how to handle such ruffians. She put 'em in their place straightaway.

"Hey there, Baby Doll," one of the more obnoxious ones sneered, "let's see what you've got! I'll bet anything them's a nice pair of knockers!"

Tillie turned to the jerk in question and quipped, "Gee, thanks for the compliment, Hon, but to you they're No Man's Land. *Capeesh*? No touchy-feely, Bub." To add insult to injury, she proclaimed, "Besides, you ain't got anything I want anyway." Her eyes hovered around the idiot's crotch area and she snickered.

The drunkards often had to be removed by force. That's where I came in, actin' in my dual role as piano player and club bouncer. Tillie knew precisely how to turn it on and off. In between her dance numbers, she'd stroll on over and visit me at the table where I took my smokin' break. Man, I can tell ya she had a body that wouldn't quit! Her face was so smooth and pretty. She loved showin' off her rosy red cheeks and those luscious red lips o' hers! Everything about her was just grand. Yesiree, she had a perfect hourglass figure, a real knockout.

Tillie was her usual charming self when it came to her relationship with me. "Care for a cig, Tillie?" I asked.

"Oh, thanks, Sweetie," she chirped, "don't mind if I do." She waved her empty cigarette holder around erratically.

"Here, let me stick this into that holder of yours, my love."

"My love?!" she shot back, flashing those beautiful eyes of hers. "Ain't you gettin' a bit too familiar with me, Buster?"

"With you it's a cinch. And I love the part 'bout familiarity." I struck a match and lit her cig.

Tillie fluttered her eyelashes at me. She drew closer, and her smile captured me like a magnet. Sitting there with her lovely smile and the cigarette smoke swirling around her, she quipped, "Y'know, Jim, if you keep talkin' this way t' me, I might wind up in the sack with you." She began playing footsies with me, and I didn't mind one bit. It continued for several minutes and I didn't have a reaction, one way or the other. "Say," she burst out, "whad'ya want to do, make me play footsies all night? I'm a big girl and don't mess around with these kids' games."

I smiled. "You have a unique way of expressing yourself, my little turtle dove."

Rolling her eyes, she exclaimed, "Oh please, Jim, you're gettin' too mushy for me. I don't like my men to get too fancy-schmantzy. Just cut out that kind o' jazz!"

I grabbed her hand and stared at her pointblank. "Well, I just hope you didn't have any trouble with those rabble-rousers who were in here earlier."

Tillie, waving away my comment, replied, "Don't worry 'bout me, Jimbo. I know how to handle them drunken bums. Next time they wanna start somethin' I'll kick 'em in the groin with these little toe-tappers o' mine!"

I tried to calm Tillie down, for I could see she was becoming agitated and excited. Those are dames for ya! "Don't work yerself into a tizzy, Babe," I admonished her. "You still have another set to perform before the night ends."

Flustered, Tillie said, "I know, I know. You don't have to remind me how even the good men in the joint don't always see my good side, just the bad, y'know? That's just part and parcel of this biz. No matter how I feel, the show must go on, as the stupid sayin' goes."

The chitchat continued for a few minutes. I glanced at my watch and said, "Looks like time for you to hit the stage again, Hon." I lifted her cig out of the holder and snuffed it out in an ashtray.

"Thanks, darlin'," she cooed, "you're a sweetie pie."

"Hmm…" I pondered aloud, "and you had the nerve to call *me* mushy?"

"Yeah, right," Tillie replied, "but you are a sweet dear anyhow. You know how to treat a lady and make her feel at home."

I offered to assist her onto the stage. I got everyone's attention in the club when we walked arm in arm and, upon letting her loose, shouted, "Here she is, ladies and gentlemen, that heart-stealer herself, Tillie." The band struck up, wailing and jiving like never before. Tillie opened the set with a solo number:

No one to talk with
All by myself
No one to walk with
But I'm happy
On the shelf
Ain't misbehavin'
I'm savin' my love for you…

The audience was impressed with her interpretation and applauded wildly. The remaining dancers filed onto the stage and accompanied her in her next number:

> *You're the cream in my coffee*
> *You're the salt in my stew*
> *You'll always be my necessity*
> *I'd be lost without you*
>
> *You're the starch in my collar*
> *You're the lace in my shoe*
> *You'll always be my necessity*
> *I'd be lost without you.*

The chorines gyrated more energetically than ever. Tillie stepped aside and allowed them to take their bows to the audience members who clapped, hooted and screamed their approval. Letting them depart, she stepped meekly to the front of the stage and accepted the audience's applause for herself alone. A standing ovation! That was something never seen before in this club. Tillie and the chorus disappeared from view. I suppose they had to go back to their dressing room to change. Near closing time, Tillie approached me as the patrons made their way to the exit. She wore a plain but attractive dress of light gray which hugged her body and accentuated every curve.

"Hi, Hon," she purred, "care to walk this poor lonely girl home? We can have a drink or two back at my place."

I perked up, never having expected a gal to be so

forward and make a proposal like this to a guy like me. "Sounds great. There's nothin' like a nightcap to round out a perfect day."

Her hand was soft to the touch as she held mine to lead me out. On the boulevard the lights of the city were dimming in the early morn. The moon shone full, and all the stars in the indigo sky seemed brighter than I could remember. This late night was the beginning of our smokin' hot love affair.

We held hands and swayed to the cool breeze of the late night/early morning quiet. Our eyes were fixed on one another, for the love bug had definitely bitten us. We finally reached the Brunswick Hotel where Tillie had a room of her own. It was a convenient location from the club. A doorman stood, rousing himself from apparent sleep, and assisted us through the hotel's revolving door. Tillie asked me, "Could you wait a sec for me to check with the reception t' see if any messages were left for me?"

We both glanced toward that area of the lobby, but since it was so late there was no one to attend to reception. Tillie smiled and said, "Oh well, I'll do it later in the day."

Tillie hurried me along to the elevator. I noticed buttons for twelve floors. "This is a pretty ritzy place here, Hon," I exclaimed.

In a cocky manner, Tillie replied, "Yeah, it is. Nothin' but the best for yours truly. I wanna live in the manner I yearn to be accustomed to, y'know?" As the elevator car went up to the eighth floor, we necked passionately and our hands were out of control as they moved up and down our fully clothed yet prematurely aroused bodies.

We got out of the elevator, with Tillie leading me as I followed. We held hands and walked briskly down the carpeted hallway until we reached room 804. She fumbled with her key opening the door, and I didn't help her composure much when I gave her a little pat on the rump.

Tillie jiggled the lock, threw the door open and flipped a light switch. To my surprise she gave me an equal little pat on my own behind. And she didn't stop there: she felt around my crotch and located the bulge in my trousers where my dick was hanging. I helped her off with her wrap while removing my coat and loosening my tie. I noticed a small divan covered in leopard skin.

"D'ya care to share a drinkie-poo with me?" she asked, fluttering her eyelashes seductively. "I have a few bottles stored away for special occasions. Have a seat, Hon." The temperature in the cold room was rising rapidly like wheat cakes on a griddle, for the atmosphere was hot with possibilities. "What's yer poison?"

"Bourbon on the rocks is my favorite. Y'got any ice, Lover?"

"Hell no! What kinda joint d'ya think this is?" she snapped. "I'm rather limited here. I'll give you two fingers in this glass. Then you can pop my girdle and unloosen my bra strap, Big Boy. That's *my* favorite."

I grinned, grabbed the glass with the two fingers of bourbon and she sat closer to me with her own glass as we sipped. Soon we put our glasses aside and began necking again.

"Oooh," she purred, "I'm so tired, and it's so late. I need a big husky fella like you to escort me to my *boudoir*. Are you up to it, Handsome?"

I smiled and replied, "I'll do you better than just escortin'. I'll give you what I like to refer to as a Pick-Me-Up."

"A Pick-Me-Up? What's that, sweetie?"

Before she could catch her breath, I cradled her and swept her off her feet, carrying her in what I assumed was the direction of her bedroom. Lowering her gently, she marveled, "My, you *are* the strong one, ain'tcha?" She gave my aroused cock, still trousered, a playful tug. Slipping out of her loosened bra and panties, her beautiful eyes glistened with an unequalled sheen.

"Looks like ya got yerself one big hammer there, Slim Jim. D'ya care to nail me down?"

I did a double-take. "Y'mean you're eager for a roll in the hay with me?"

Nodding, she said, "You bet, Big Jim --- and I do mean *big*!"

We both squeezed and held one another tightly. We felt as free as wildcats. I could hear Tillie purring like a kitten. Man, this dame sure was hot to trot! She reached down, sticking her hand behind my belt and into my pants, giving my prick a few hearty tugs.

"Hey, Jimmy Poo," she quipped saucily, "I think it's high time you mount this toe-tapping gal. This is the moment of truth, lover. Gimme all you've got, Honey Pot."

Visions of saddling up and taking this wild filly for a ride danced in my head. The more she touched me and talked so provocatively, the harder and firmer I became. I was aroused to the breaking point. Clothes came off without us realizing their removal, and we positioned ourselves on Tillie's plush bed. Tillie demonstrated that she was no innocent filly, but instead turned into a flaming hot mare. I humped her like a stray tomcat and we thrashed unbridled as two adults in the throes of lust.

In a matter of minutes Tillie cried out in ecstasy. Even in this breathless moment, she was her usual feisty self. "Did ya shoot yer load, Buddy Boy?" she sneered as I nodded, smiling. "I know you made me reach my peak, Jimbo." We relaxed our bodies and soon fell asleep in each other's arms.

Neither of us stirred until close to ten o'clock that morning entwined in one another. This was the first of several of our "hot dates," and I could tell that the situation between us was gettin' more serious each time we got together. I was crazy about that chick, but she had a side to her that frankly I didn't see comin'.

That week I planned on popping the big question to her. I wanted to spend the rest of my born days with that sexy dame. She was my doll, my love bunny. I decided to go ahead with it on a Saturday night.

Something was about to unfold prior to the evening we got together for our usual performance at the club. I noticed a young man in the darkened crowd. I gotta admit, the guy was better lookin' than me. I realized I couldn't turn back the hands of time to be in my twenties again. That was the age range of this particular young pup. And what a hoity-toity type he was, a real flashy dresser. And the guy exuded a certain air 'bout hisself. He'd make me look like a slob if you stood us side by side.

When Tillie came onstage, the young man fixated on her, not diverting his eyes for a second. She normally grabbed people's attention, but this guy was devouring her with his stare in a way I'd never seen before. Tillie and the girls had performed several numbers. When it was their cue to take a break, the young man lost no time waving Tillie over to where he was sitting. Obviously Tillie had noticed him in the crowd and completely ignored me, sitting with her new discovery for over ten minutes, chatting and carrying on in a kittenish manner.

Then it hit me. "That's Frank Cordova," I gasped. "He's the biggest, brashest young owner of a recording company here in New York." I could only guess what they were talking about. It didn't look like business, but who knows? "There's more than meets the eye with this intruder," I thought to myself.

Tillie showed me a side of herself I hadn't seen before. She seemed very impressionable to me, and a bit picky. I was within an earshot of where she sat with him and overheard part of their conversation when the patrons of the club had quieted down a bit.

"Hey, that show you did up there was great," Cordova said. "You'll go far in this biz. And since I own the largest record company here in Manhattan, I can arrange for you to come to the studio and take part in a session with a few of my best musicians."

Tillie smiled in a way I'd never seen before. It was like witnessing a fireworks display. "Gee, Mister Cordova," she squealed, "that's just dandy."

Interrupting her by putting his hand up, he insisted, "Please don't call me Mister Cordova. It's 'Frank' to you from now on."

Tillie smiled. "Okay, Frank," she responded obediently. "I'll do whatever you say."

I couldn't help noticing how fresh he started getting with her, placing his hand on top of hers and holding it with their fingers entwined for several minutes. I had the urge to stroll over to where they sat and give him a piece of my mind, even punching his lights out if necessary. I held back, not wanting to cause a scene, and certainly not desiring to embarrass Tillie.

I caught a little more of their flirtatious conversation. "Y'know, I really like you, Tillie," Cordova exclaimed.

In a throwaway manner, Tillie replied, "Yeah, the

feelin's mutual." Then with a bit more seriousness, she added, "I think I could fall for a guy like you, big time! To be perfectly honest, Frank, I prefer my men to have class and social standin', ya get my drift? You've got them things in spades, everything I love in a man."

From the way he was talking and the manner in which she responded, I knew what was coming next. "You don't happen to have any other boyfriends or love interests, do you, Tillie?"

Tillie shook her head and pouted. "Not really," she murmured. "There's one guy, but now that you asked me, I don't think he's serious enough to wanna commit. 'sides, he ain't got much class."

Frank Cordova chuckled. "Oh, Tillie," he said, "you've certainly got a way with words. You have what it takes to bowl a guy over, even someone like me who's eminently successful and could have his pick of any woman he wants. If you've got the time after you're through in this dump, I'd like to take you out so we can paint the town together. We'll hit all the swankiest spots before the sun comes up. What do you say?"

Tillie couldn't refuse an offer like that, I feared. Mister Hot-to-Trot, the man who stole my Tillie and everything I had planned for her, had finally shown up.

"I'm ready to go now," Tillie asserted. "I don't have any more sets tonight. It's time for us to blow this joint." She stood up and, still holding hands tightly with Frank, off they went into the night. I never saw or heard from her again except for a telegram shoved under my door at the boarding house one night:

Sorry, Hon STOP
Better offer from younger man STOP
Couldn't turn him down STOP
Love Tillie

Slim Jim snaps out of his dreamlike state and looks at us directly again. Lighting a cigarette and taking a long drag, he laments his bygone memories.

"I sit here alone. That gal went and stole my heart. Me and her would've been great together, but who knows? After what she did to me, I'm glad I found out sooner than later. What a big heartbreaker she turned out to be. She dropped me like a sack of potatoes, just like that! I'm convinced they'll never be another women like her in my life."

Sneering, he adds, "I wish Frank and Tillie a happy life together; they deserve each other." Taking a last puff and snuffing out half the cigarette, he straightens up and speaks boldly like a man wounded in spirit.

"Yesiree --- there sure wasn't a dish tastier than that Tillie of mine. But you'll have to excuse me: I gotta get back to the business of playin' my music. In the mood I'm in, I'm gonna pound them keys like never before and sing like there's no tomorrow!

I can be happy, I can be sad
I can be good or I can be bad
It all depends on you

I can be lonely out in a crowd
I can be humble, I can be proud
It all depends on you

I can save money, or spend it
Go right on living, or end it
You're to blame, honey, for what I do

I know that
I can be beggar, I can be king
I can be almost any old thing
It all depends on you....

FRANK CORDOVA GETS THE SHAFT

When I first laid eyes on this incredibly swinging gal she left me dumbfounded. I couldn't keep those eyes of mine off her for a second. She had a magnificent feminine, almost feline presence. I met her one night at the *Diamond Rose Carousel*. We met, chatted a while and I ended up carrying her away like a knight in shining armor. I had definite plans for this ravishing, seductive beauty. I promised her the world, for that's what we in show business do anyway.

In addition to my ownership of Cordova Records, I also act as talent scout and agent for up-and-coming young stars. The difference is that I'm not a phony like some of those fly-by-night characters turn out to be. My time is valuable, and so is my money. Why take the trouble to invest in some broad who doesn't have the makings of a star? A broad's got to have "it," and believe me, Tillie had "it."

My plans for her were vast, but she ended up wanting even more than what was in my power and influence to do for her. I hate to admit it, since I'm a fairly intelligent fellow, but she took me for a ride, and ended up cleaning me out. Her charm and allure had me over a barrel. She spent her money *and* mine like it was going out of style. She demanded the finest of everything. "Only the best for Tillie," was her motto.

When she paraded around in her new dresses and

frocks I was mesmerized. She would suddenly take on the air of a high-class society dame. She figured out how she'd fleece me just by knowing my status and wealth. After all, it isn't every day that she met the owner of a talent agency and recording company. The idea pulled on the money-grubbing strings of her heart, and she suddenly had dollars signs in her eyes.

I took a personal interest in her, enabling her to get the finest of training. I hired a dance instructor named Linda Weisenheimer to refine Tille's natural talents and prepare her for stage appearances in conjunction with the recordings I had in mind. I desired to elevate her to the big time: no more gin joints or smoke-filled speakeasies for Tillie, just the cream of the crop nightclubs, salons and big venues.

I knew that Linda could pull this off, since she herself had performed in the chorus line, starting at the bottom during her own career. She was at the summit of her accomplishments. I introduced her to Tillie, and they hit it off perfectly.

"You know, Tillie," Linda said, "we girls have a certain style and allure to all of our movements. We attract male customers."

Tilled grinned and responded, "Don't I know it! I had to put up with a whole bunch o' them stage door johnnies at the joints I used t' work at."

Linda arched her eyebrows and shot back, "Well, Tillie, you're leaving all that behind and hitting the big time now. Frank'll fill you in with more details about the plans he has for you."

Tillie's face perked up and she smiled as if radiant sunshine were streaming through her. From that day on, Linda gave her thorough lessons in limbering up and performing all the latest dance crazes. When two weeks of training had passed, Frank paid her a visit.

"Hey there, Tillie," he called out as she was finishing one of the routines Linda had devised for her. When she heard her name, she rushed over to him with wings on her feet. They kissed each other and flirted playfully. "Linda tells me you're fabulous. You'll be ready for your first big show in no time at all."

"Gee, Frankie pumpkin," she cooed coquettishly, "d'ya wanna tell me where that'll be?"

Frank smiled and replied, "At the *Grand Emporium* in the heart of Manhattan. Your name'll be in lights since you're gonna be the main attraction. All I have to do to round out your training is hook you up with a voice coach to hone your already natural singing talent. The guy's name is Tony Benson, and he's the best in the biz."

Tillie brightened. "Oh, I know 'im," she gushed. "He's a real heart throb. Ya really think he can help a gal like me?"

"Sure," Frank asserted. "He has both male and female clients."

In a couple of days Tony Benson visited Tillie. He began her instruction and soon realized that she was his favorite client. Tillie also burned with lust for the handsome voice coach who'd reportedly broken many a female heart. He readied her in no time for her début at the *Grand Emporium.* The marquee blazed brightly with her name on that fateful Saturday evening.

I'll never forget the packed crowd we had on opening night. Everyone in the audience was really ready to jump and jive. I peeked through the curtain to the stage. Two thousand or more excited people stared back in my direction, and boy, were they ever hoppin'! The lights dimmed, and as I walked out to introduce her to everyone the spotlight followed me.

"Ladies and Gentlemen," I began, "thanks for coming out tonight. I'm Frank Cordova, but I'm not the one you came to see, so I won't flap my yap too much. Without further ado, I invite you to sit back, get comfortable and enjoy these swingin', flingin' flappers, the gem of gems, The Damettes!"

The chorus girls commenced the warm-up act, dancing on stage with their version of the Black Bottom. After five full minutes of wild, uninhibited gyrations, they took their bows and welcomed me back on stage.

"Man, weren't those dames the cat's meow?" I asked the crowd, and another round of applause filled the air. "And now I have the pleasure of introducing you to my most recent discovery, and what a discovery she was --- wow, wow, wow! She's the one you've come to see in her début performance here. Ladies and Gents, here's our star of tonight's show, the One and Only Tillie!"

The Emporium darkened and the shadow of a small figure emerged onto the massive stage. The spotlight was aimed in such a way that only the top of her head showed. A silken cap trimmed with diamonds bedazzled the crowd. They went completely bonkers when the light streamed lower to highlight her smiling face, offset by a pair of long glittering earrings. Her glitzy dress was stunning, all covered in sequins and shiny baubles. The effect was virtually blinding. The length was not too short to offend nor too long to detract from the perfect shape of her legs. Her tap shoes were also covered in dazzling jewels of many colors.

Two tuxedoed chorus boys waltzed toward her from opposite ends of the stage, one carrying a huge feather boa while the other wielded a giant fan made of peacock plumes in various colors. Tillie bid the two boys to exit, stepped boldly forward and soaked in the attention of the crowd. Blowing a kiss to them, she immediately she launched into the first song on the program:

> *Ma, he's makin' eyes at me*
> *Ma, he's awful nice to me*
> *Ma, he's breaking my heart*
> *I'm beside him*
> *Mercy, let his conscience guide him*

Ma, he wants to marry me,
Be my honey bee….

Applause rang through the *Grand Emporium* as Tillie sang the last note. Without missing a beat, the band struck up again and she sailed right into her second number. Punctuating each bar of the new song, the band members shouted out, "Hep, hep!" Tillie smiled coyly and let loose with the lyrics:

Jim Jam,
Jump the Jumpin' Jive
Cat's gonna beat out
this mellow jive…

The saucy tone of the words sung by a sweet ingénue as well as the continued shouts of "Hep, hep!" from the band members were something that hadn't ever been seen on this stage.

As the loud applause and shouts of approval subsided, Tillie looked out into the audience and felt a rush of excitement at being the center of attention by so many thousands of strangers. Approaching the standup microphone, she gushed, "Thank you all ever so much. You're all a bunch of sweetie pies!" She threw additional kisses to the crowd and the show continued uninterrupted with many more musical numbers.

Near the end of the set, the Damettes joined her

in demonstrating the Charleston as it had never been danced before. They broke into little groups surrounding Tillie who also shook and shimmied to the rhythms of the band's fiery notes. I even came out myself, sporting a striped jacket, straw boater and a cane which I twirled expertly. I was so caught up in Tillie's performance that I hardly realized what a bopping fool I must have looked like.

"Let's give the Damettes a round of applause!" I shouted. The crowd responded in kind. "And, last but not least, please show appreciation and love for our star Tillie!"

The following morning I browsed through the various trade publications on my local newsstand. *Variety*'s banner headline read "Newcomer is Socko Sensation at Emporium." A tabloid paper, *Manhattan Gossip*, and the entertainment section of the *New York Times* all featured glowing reviews about her performance. Even though it was a little past dawn, I rang up Tillie to give her the good news. She was drowsy when she lifted the receiver, but suddenly perked up.

"Wow, Frank," she squeaked, "you're sendin' my heart in a whirl, a toe-tappin' fluttery spin, Doll." I promised to catch up with her later in the day, making a date for lunch at the *Wildcats Café*. I intended to bring her a new surprise, something which I'd been keeping under wraps --- you might say, under my derby.

She'd beat me to the café. Standing outside and

attracting the attention of passersby, her eyes lit up when she saw me approach from the opposite side of Fifth Avenue. A maître d' escorted us to a secluded table, away from the crowded main room and out of sight from nosey parkers. Tillie was as excited as a little girl at a birthday party. I laid out the papers for her and pointed to the reviews I had circled.

"Well now, Tillie," I began, "feast your eyes on these kind words from New York's finest critics."

Tillie read a line or two, picking out the more complimentary, sensational words and phrases. Blinking, she exclaimed, "Gee, it looks like they all have grand taste, huh?" I perceived a prideful attitude in this young lady. I smiled and nodded anyway.

"I've saved an even bigger surprise for you, my sweet," I said.

Tillie's eyes grew wider. "How could you possibly surprise me any more than this?" she responded, pointing to the reviews still laid out all over the table. "Where is it? Where are you hiding it?" Shaking her head in a playful manner, she added, "It ain't nothin' naughty, is it?"

I burst into laughter. I took off my derby and removed a rolled-up sleeve of paper. "Look here, Tillie," I explained, "this is a contract I've drawn up. It entitles you to perform exclusively at the *Grand Emporium* for the next three years." I smiled confidently, but wasn't ready for her reaction.

"Three measly years?!" she blurted. Her face turned dark and menacing. "Is that all? Why, I deserve more than *that*! Accordin' to these reviews, I'm the hottest thing goin' in New York. And when you're hot to trot like me, you gotta give me more than three crummy years at that joint."

It was at that moment that a frightening though flashed through my mind. "My God," I shuddered, "what kind of monster have I created?" As smart and crafty as I was, I could never have guessed what was to come from the treacherous web this black widow could weave.

Tillie's shows continued to be a roaring success, filling the *Grand Emporium* nightly without fail. My next step was to book a few dates for her in the recording studio, as we had previously discussed. It was there that her singing voice could garner an even larger and wider outreach. I instructed her to meet me at the entrance to my recording company, jotting down all the information she needed to know and handing it to her one evening after another stellar performance onstage. In her usual coquettish way, she was stimulated beyond measure.

"I'll slay 'em with my beautiful voice," she quipped. "Wait'll those record buyers out there get a load of this singin' dame. I'll have 'em eatin' out o' my hand, right?" She strutted around her dressing room with her nose high in the air and swirling her feather boa. "I'll be the talk of the continent, maybe the whole wide world. I wanna be known as 'Tillie, the Golden-Throated Wonder of the Century.' There ain't gonna be need for any of them other broads. When ya got me," she sneered, "you can forget you sweet ass about Ruth Etting, Vaughn deLeath and Annette Hanshaw. Between 'em there ain't a quarter of the talent I have."

I smiled benignly. "So I guess I can count of you, Tillie," I said with a catch in my voice.

"Yeah," she replied, "I'll be there with bells on." She gave me her now infamous peck on the cheek as well as the equally infamous pat on my butt.

"You're pretty sure of yourself, my dear."

"Of course I am, Lover Boy. When you're hot, you're hot. So don't get yer li'l ol' fingers burned, sweetie."

"You've proven that every night here at the *Grand Emporium* is a magical evening, no doubt about it."

Tillie sniffed. "You can say that again, Mister Butt Cakes," she giggled. "I can slap 'em 'til the cows come home. I'll warm them buns up for you."

I escorted her back to her hotel. She had changed rooms, moving up to the penthouse with a maid and personal chef. The luxurious atmosphere of the suite was conducive to intense lovemaking, enough to last an entire night or more.

I rushed Tillie and Tony Benson into the building which housed my recording studio on a miserable rainy day in New York. I looked like a drenched cat after emerging from the taxi and running for the entrance, while Tillie and Tony breezed in, quite dry and apparently unfazed by the pelt of raindrops. I had convinced Tony to come along for moral support, though I perceived Tillie was more than confident, almost conceited as to the validity of her performing talents. Her show at the *Grand Emporium* had been held over for another six months. At every supper club and upscale speakeasy where she appeared, she was asked by the bandleader to sing a number or two for the assembled multitudes. She always obliged, though she usually cut it off after two songs because she didn't like spoiling her evenings out.

I walked Tillie through the entire record pressing routine, demonstrating the way the microphone would pick up her voice as the orchestra accompanied her singing. I described in detail the way the needle would transfer the recorded material onto hot shellac and transform the disc into a prototype for the pressing of duplicate phonograph records. She feigned interest, but seemed bored, not even suppressing a yawn as she clutched Tony by the arm.

"Jeesh," she finally said, rolling her eyes and throwing up her hands, "can't we just get the hell on with it? You're borin' me to death with all this needless explanation. I just wanna sing a couple o' songs and blow so's I can get back to the penthouse for a little party I'm throwin' later tonight."

I stared at Tillie in dismay. She hadn't told me about any party at her penthouse. This was the first

I'd heard about it, and I must say I was a little hurt that she hadn't thought about inviting me. After all, I had been so instrumental in launching her entire career. She ignored me, instead making goo-goo eyes at Tony, practically staring holes in him.

"Alright, Tillie," I replied sheepishly, "just give me a minute or two to consult with the recording booth so we can set up a sound check or two."

Tillie shot a look at me that I can only describe as hateful. "Whadya mean, sound check?" she sneered. "Quit wastin' time and let's get on with it."

It was all I could do to keep my temper under control. Taking a deep breath, I began, "It's not a question of getting on with it, my dear. This equipment you see around you is very sensitive. It can pick up the slightest breath or little variance in pitch, and you don't want to transfer any of that kind of nonsense to your recordings. People'll buy these records and hear any imperfections. Then they won't want to hear your songs anymore if there are too many mistakes due to our negligence. Does that make sense to you, sweetie?"

Tillie hung onto Tony more tightly than ever. He caressed the sleeve of her mink coat and provided a level of comfort I was unable to muster. "I dunno," she said sullenly. "All this don't seem t' be worth my time and effort." Looking up lovingly at Tony, she asked, "Whadya you say, Babe?"

I was put off by her affection for Tony, but kept my cool. Reassuringly, he explained to her, "Frank's right, though. If you want to be at your best and have the needle imprinting the shellac to duplicate your voice with its finest quality, you've got to do a couple of voice checks prior to singing the songs in their entirety."

Thank goodness Tony was able to put it in terms better than I could have. Tillie shrugged, seemed to be resigned to the sound check idea and replied, "Alright, Tony, you're the boss. I'll put up with it."

I did a double take. I was under the impression I was the boss, but again said nothing. I was an anxious to get this whole thing over with as quickly as possible. Tillie's behavior with Tony was getting on my nerves, too.

I need not have worried about the voice check or Tillie's singing ability as transmitted to sound recording. I am happy to say she was a natural and we were able to knock out several songs in no time. The members of the accompanying orchestra were smitten with Tillie's playful nature. She conveyed a great deal of personality in her recordings. And the songs which had been written exclusively for her were superbly interpreted, largely due to the band members' ability to improvise around Tillie's amazing voice. Her first big hit sold more than a million copies throughout America:

You're so hotsy-totsy,
You give me the vapors,
You're the cat's meow,

It's in all the papers,
You're the man o' my dreams
Fulfillin' all o' my schemes
You're that hotsy-totsy
Sweet ol' honey o' mine...

And who could forget this gem...

If you treat me bad
You're gonna make me sad
Be good t' your dear ol' mammy
'cause I think you're just the cat's pyjammy.
Listen closely to what I say
Before I up and run away
You naughty boy, you!

That song was played on the radio and caused record sales to go through the roof both in this country as well as worldwide. Tillie received fan mail from people living far west as California and as far east as Istanbul. Marriage proposals came in from princes, dukes and ordinary folks. One distraught Arabian sheik threatened to commit suicide if Tillie didn't come to his desert oasis and become the thirtieth bride in his harem of wives and concubines.

Tillie, to her credit, was too busy to see most of this fan mail because she had become the darling of New York society. She had accepted an invitation from a wealthy admirer who lived out on Long Island, spending an entire weekend with him in the luxurious splendor of his sprawling estate and performing one of her latest numbers for the attendees of a lavish party he threw in her honor:

Shower me with diamonds,
I'll belong to you forever.
Give me mink and ermine,
I'll promise to leave you never.
Put a million in my account
And buy me shares on margin,
I'll be your lovin' sweetie
Believe me, that's some bargain!

Tillie really had it made, becoming an international as well as national success. And yet she was not fully satisfied. It was still my hope that I could bring a level of happiness and contentment to this gorgeous dame. I even purchased a glittering three-karat diamond ring. Surely she'd be impressed with that, and it would make us both happy.

You've probably guessed by now that I'd fallen madly in love with her. There was one special occasion which stands out in my memory: the night I intended to propose marriage to her. I invited her to my place out in Westchester County. I still owned a mansion there, but because of my work in town I seldom inhabited it. But this event was the exception. I had an entire staff of maids, servants and cooks who attended to my every need when I was in residence. I admired their professional, proficient way of doing things.

Around seven o'clock in the evening on what was to be the special date, Tillie arrived in a limousine I had sent for her. She was met at the front door by my butler. I soon followed, greeting her warmly and giving her a kiss, to which she barely yielded.

"How are you tonight, Tillie?" I asked, indicating the luxurious surroundings. "What do you think of my little home away from home?"

Tillie sniffed, waved her cigarette holder in a carefree, lackadaisical manner and dryly replied, "Hmmph…, I guess it'll do." Moving her eyes to and fro in a nonchalant way, she added, "Nice joint ya got here, Sugar."

I was surprised and taken aback by her reaction. I expected her to be a bit more impressed. With Tillie, however, anything was possible. She could be flighty at times, and it was difficult to pin her down. It would have been easier to tame a wild horse. A servant removed her coat and I proceeded to take her on a brief tour of my place.

"I ain't gonna lie to ya," Tillie said, "I gotta admit this is a classy place, Sweetums." From that moment on I realized she was beginning to warm up to me and the idea of wedded bliss. I led her to the vast garden at the rear of the mansion. Under the setting sun I showed her all the wonders supplied by Mother Nature. The first thing that caught her attention was not the neatly arranged flower beds, but rather the swimming pool.

"Ooh," she squealed, "that's a mighty fine swimmin' hole, Babe. I wouldn't mind divin' into it sometime." Removing her shoe and approaching the rim of the pool, she asked, "Ya ain't got nothin' against me puttin' my foot in there a little just to get my tootsie wet, do ya?" Upon doing so, she shrieked, "Golly, that water sure is icy cold! Whadya tryin' do, make a gal freeze?"

Shaking my head, I responded, "Oh no, I'd never do anything like that. I like you just the way you are, Tillie: so warm, wonderful and cuddly. Not frozen at all." I chuckled, but Tillie just stared at me blankly.

I informed my butler to prepare a tray with two glasses of brandy to be served in my boudoir. He nodded obsequiously, and I proceeded to escort Tillie upstairs. After the requested tray was presented, the butler departed in a timely manner.

"I thought this would be a nice idea to welcome you," I began, "sort of a way kick things off."

Tillie giggled. "Hmm…," she purred, "I'd adore kickin' things off with you anytime, Mister Long Dong." She caught me speechless with such affectionate talk, and we both burst out laughing.

Things became even looser as the one glass of brandy, then another and another were consumed. I waddled over to a chest of drawers at the opposite end of my bed chamber. I quickly opened a cabinet and brought out a small velvet-lined box. Staggering back over to Tillie, I asked her to close her eyes.

"Hey," she exclaimed, "whadya pullin'? Why the

hell should I close my baby blues?" Continuing to pout, she added, "You ain't gonna tell me ya got some kind o' weird lookin' pecker, are ya?"

Chuckling, I replied, "Heavens no, my dear child. I have something much more useful and lovelier than that for you."

Tillie stared at me intensely. "Well, what could be lovelier than a double roll in the hay? Answer me that, wise guy!"

I brought out the little box and with a flourish proclaimed, "Ta-da!" Her eyes opened wide, and she could scarcely believe what she was looking at.

"Oh gosh," she cried, "it's a diamond ring. Oh, quick! Slip it on my finger right away. I wanna admire it!"

"You are now the proud owner of a three-karat diamond, Tillie," I said proudly. Suddenly a blank expression crossed her face.

"Three lousy karats?" she screamed. "Whadya take me for, some kind o' schnook?"

Shaking my head, I reflected, "Oh well, that plan fell through. It figures. That sounds just like my Tillie." I threw myself on top of her anyway and we wiggled around on the silk bedspread. In spite of her indifference, I decided to pop the big question anyway.

"Tillie," I said breathlessly, "I'm nuts about you. Will you do me the honor of becoming my wife?"

Still squirming wildly and struggling to release herself from my grasp, she responded with resignation, "Oh, alright, ya big lummox. I'll marry ya!"

I hugged and kissed her madly. We acted like a couple of polecats in heat. Even Tillie was making the most of our little fling.

"Gee," she put forth at breakfast the following morning, "we sure had us one helluva time last night, huh? That hot tamale of yours sure was nice, Honey Bun." Fluttering her eyelashes, she added, "Nice and spicy, the way I like it!"

I smiled and responded jovially, "Your pair o' tacos ain't too shabby either, Tillie." I perceived she didn't care for my tongue-in-cheek approach, so I switched back to being serious. "I'm happy to know that they'll be all mine, now and forevermore." With breakfast concluded we strolled through the garden and discussed our wedding plans in depth. We set the date for August 2nd at three o'clock.

"Would you like a church wedding, Tillie?" I asked.

"Nuh-uh," she answered nonchalantly, "I ain't that religious. 'sides, them church types give me the heebie-jeebies."

Disappointed but trying not to be too obvious, I suggested, "What do you say to putting on a ceremony here in the garden? We'll keep the invitation list restricted and let in only those who are close friends. I know a local minister who can perform the wedding. He's Episcopalian and we've been acquainted for years. He was born in England, but he came over here ten years ago. He's known as the Reverend Stiffwilly, Senior."

Tillie looked aghast. "Stiffwilly?" she cried. "Whatsamatta with 'im? He ain't deformed or anything like that, is he?"

I patted her hand and said reassuringly, "Never fear, my sweet. That's just his name, though I have to admit it is a bit strange. After all, he was born and raised in London, willy and all."

Smiling thinly and rolling her eyes, she quipped sarcastically, "I can only imagine what the poor slob must've gone through all his life."

I made all of the last minute plans for our wedding. I noticed that Tillie wasn't as thrilled as I was. I never doubted my undying love for her, and I hoped she felt the same way. The intensity didn't seem to be there, but shucks, I was probably just imagining things.

One afternoon something so strange took place, I couldn't put my finger on it. The incident came to me through the grapevine. People began inquiring if I knew Tillie's whereabouts. It occurred to me that I'd also tried reaching her several times, without success.

One old biddy, an acquaintance of mine who I considered fairly narrow-minded, sneered, "I saw that hussy out with a whole bunch of other men, drinking, cavorting and acting like a brazen whore."

I refused to believe it until Tillie finally showed up a few nights later in my living room. She had stumbled in initially, though she began building up steam to such an extent that she danced and pranced with abandon through the house and out into the garden. I could only describe her face as vacuous, no expression. She reminded me of one of those deadpan comics you'd often see in the flickers.

"Tillie dear," I asked meekly, approaching her without making any sudden movements, "where in Heaven's name have you been? I've been trying to reach you. Everybody's been worried about you."

Lifting her eyes sleepily and grinning, she slurred her reply, "Eh, nowhere much. Just with a bunch o' pals o' mine. There's nothin' like a swingin' crowd to lift my spirits, y'know." Wiping her lips with the back of her hand, she added, "Why d'ya ask? You ain't jealous or nothin', are ya? I ain't gone and tied the knot with ya yet, so don't hold me down, Buster. I'm still a freewheelin' dame, free as a little bird."

I stood before her, thunderstruck. Then she blurted out, "So when ya gonna gimme my weddin' dress, Big Boy?" She swiveled her hips with a definite grind and placed a heavy hand on my shoulder. "Ya better send over a hairdresser while yer at it. I need to get this mop o' mine washed and curled."

Speechless, I continued staring at her in disbelief. Adding insult to injury, she chirped, "So whadya standin' there for like ya got yer head up yer ass? Get a move on, Sherlock! While yer at it, tell that dishy chauffeur o' yours I gotta make a run into town later on today. I'm goin' to Tiffany's to do a li'l shoppin'. I'll tell 'em to charge everythin' t' you, Babe. If you wanna keep me happy, better cooperate or you'll lose me, yer li'l love bundle."

The big day had come with all its pomp and intricately prepared details. Tillie and I had just finished breakfast, and she was all smiles. This was not usual, for at times leading up to the big day I caught her off-guard with a look of dismay or total vacancy. Her face was like that of a clown, but without expression.

"Well, Tillie," I leaned over and spoke low, "this is it. Are you ready for the biggest, best and greatest day of your life?"

She pulled back for a second, looked confused, then suddenly a light seemed to come on. "Oh, yeah," she replied in a cool manner, "this is when you told me I'm getting' hitched t' ya."

I grinned and said coyly, "Tying the knot, so to speak."

"I guess that's right, Frankie boy."

"Are you ready, my dear?"

Tillie looked away, so far away that I felt she wasn't even with me. "Hmm," she murmured, "yeah, I s'ppose so. That kind o' thing happens ev'ry day. Just like the facts o' life, huh?"

"If you're referring to the birds and bees, Tillie, I imagine you and I are like two love birds, right?"

"Oh, I guess so. It'd be worse if we got stung by the bees, 'speci'ly on our tushes."

Abruptly, Tillie rose from her chair and snapped her fingers. "Listen, Frankie darlin'," she purred, "I just remembered I've gotta run a few last minute errands, plus check on the final fittin' for that weddin' dress ya ordered. Gotta rush," she added, looking impatiently at her watch. "Don't bother wakin' up the chauffeur. I'll take one of your cars and do everything m'self."

Disappointed, I exclaimed, "This is rather sudden, but OK, whatever you think is best, dear. The keys to the roadster are upstairs on the side table next to your room."

Tillie grinned slyly. "Oh, that's convenient, Sugar Plum." Patting me on the cheek, she said sweetly, "Hey, don't be so glum. I promise it won't take long. I'll be back here in time to get ready for the big shindig." The way she shrugged put me off a bit.

I went off to consult with the staff of the mansion about the arrangements for the ceremony and dinner to follow, scarcely noticing Tillie as she ran upstairs and not even seeing her depart in the roadster. That was around noon, so there were a little less than three hours to go before the wedding.

One o'clock came fast, then two. Guests began arriving in droves and were ushered in. The Right Reverend Stiffwilly, Senior also breezed in, all smiles and radiating charm. I continued smiling all the while, though nervous tension was creeping in as two thirty came and went, still with no Tillie in sight.

Approaching me and noticing how perturbed I was, Reverend Stiffwilly asked, "Are we to assume that the bride-to-be is still primping?"

Shrugging my shoulders, I responded, "I have no idea. She told me she would have to run a few last-minute errands. Frankly, I was so busy consulting with my staff that I failed to notice if she'd even arrived back here."

"It is usually a good idea, my dear Mister Cordova," the Right Reverend advised, "to do a welfare check in such cases. I'll hold down the fort here while you go up to check on the dear lady to whom you will very shortly be united in wedded bliss."

His British accent had a calming effect on me and I proceeded to climb the stairs. It was now fifteen minutes after three. The assembled friends, acquaintances and other invitees were becoming restless as the minutes ticked by. Hardly anyone spoke as they shifted uncomfortably in the seats laid out in rows before the flower-bedecked trellis, fidgeting and groaning.

My first call was to the dressmaker's salon. "Oh no," the sympathetic lady on the other end of the line declared, "we haven't seen her for hours." I checked a few other places where Tillie might have stopped to conduct business, but got the same answer each time: no sign of her anywhere.

Racing downstairs again, I told the staff to quickly prepare some finger food and hors d'oeuvres. I also announced that there would be a slight delay but that cocktails would be served while we waited. This brought a deluge of people springing from their seats and rushing to the bar for some of the high quality booze I'd been able to procure for the event.

A wealthy tycoon named Johnathan Meyers, the owner of big parcels of Manhattan real estate, waddled toward me with his huge belly stuffed into an ill-fitting tuxedo. "If it's not imposing on you, old man," he quipped, "I was wondering when you were planning to bring out the wedding cake."

Smirking, I replied, "Just hold your horses, Meyers. The bride-to-be is running a bit late."

The invited guests continued to gorge on the delicious appetizers and consume gallons of my booze as four thirty, then five o'clock rolled around. I was in full panic. I had no choice but to barge into Tillie's room and find out what was holding her up.

I found the door unlocked, and inside the luxuriously furnished room there wasn't hide nor hair of Tillie. While I'd been distracted with my end of the preparations for the wedding ceremony, she had flown the coop, leaving the meticulously tailored wedding dress hanging in her closet all by itself. On the nightstand the small velvet lined box I'd given her was left flipped open; the three-karat diamond ring I'd presented to her when I proposed was gone.

Holding back my anger and tears, I hazily saw a pile of discarded papers off to the side. A slightly crumpled hand-written note was perched atop:

Here are the receipts for everything I charged.
It sure came in handy when I decided

to go on a shopping spree.
As much as I love you, I can't be tied down.
There's plenty more fish in the sea.
I'm heading out and won't be back.
So long, Poopsie.

Tillie

I sat on Tillie's bed and felt mighty low. How could she have done something like this to me? Just walking out, after everything her heart desired had been given to her. I set her up to be a sensation performing live every night, and even arranged for her to record many songs, allowing her fame to spread beyond anyone's imagination. She was always the talk of the town --- every town in every corner of the world. The sky was the limit for her.

But at whose expense? Mine, of course! How could I have been so blind? She charged everything to the hilt and stuck me with the tab. What was I to do now? I had guests waiting downstairs and one big fat slob who had already asked about the wedding cake.

Trying to organize my thoughts amid the anguish of losing Tillie, I came up with a scheme. I decided to boldly inform everyone that Tillie had had a last minute change in plans, caused by an unforeseen family emergency. That's the only excuse I could come up with for a two-bit floozie like her. Her reputation had obviously proceeded her, but I was too enamored to see it, blinded by love as it were.

ROBERT WISEMAN'S SAD STORY

The sign at the entrance to one of Tinsletown's biggest studios read HOLLYWOOD CINEMA PICTURES, Incorporated. Many a big star would tootle up in his or her shiny motorcar. The biggest of the big would leave that task to a personal chauffeur. For the rest of the bit players, wannabe hopefuls and assorted stragglers, a swing gate manned by a fierce looking security guard awaited.

In its heyday many great award-winning motion pictures were turned into the magic of celluloid by the talented directors and astute producers associated with this successful studio. The silent era brought in millions of dollars to Hollywood Cinema's coffers when one box office smash after another hit the screens. *The Sheik of the Sahara Desert* was a huge moneymaker, only bested by shoot-'em-up Westerns like the infamous *Guns at High Noon* or mystery thrillers such as *The Inscrutable Doctor Wong* and *Shadows of False Face*.

I had the distinction of owning this blockbuster film corporation, along with my partners Bill Fieldmann and Herman Nettelbaum. On a daily basis we took in hundreds of thousands, and our annual reports ran into millions. As the saying goes, we were rolling in dough and there seemed to be no end to our successful venture.

I saw many people in the course of my job as studio head. I recall one actress who breezed into my office on a fateful day in 1926. At first glance she attracted all my attention, something which rarely happens because I'd become so jaded by my work and position. To moviegoers worldwide she eventually became the hottest thing going.

The first day I laid eyes on her was memorable. We were casting for a new film, *Queen of the Rubies*, the story about an Arabian beauty who fought to protect her land and precious gemstones contained therein --- mountains of rubies, diamonds and sapphires reaching to the sky. Her knights and warriors protected her from intruders and infidels. We were prepared to put everything into this production because we expected the gross receipts to be bigger than ever for a single motion picture.

A general casting call was issued. We wanted to hire a relatively unknown actress for the lead role instead of using one of the big stars of the day. Girls and women of all ages, shapes, sizes and complexions formed a huge line outside the studio, and were called in one by one for a short interview. After four hours and having spoken to a number of ladies, none of them quite fit the bill. I instructed the agents to resume auditioning the hopefuls after a lunch break, leaving scores of women still standing outside in the relatively warm sunshine.

The two hours which followed the lunch break produced nothing substantial either in the way of our future star. I was ready to tell them to scrap the whole idea when my eye caught Tillie a mere five minutes before we had scheduled to end for the day. She had definitely changed the entire atmosphere of the room when she stepped in; her look was entrancing and everything else about her was perfect. It's not often that someone draws my attention in such a big way.

I decided to handle her interview myself. "What is your name, my dear?" I asked gently.

"Tillie Thompson," she answered, showing two rows of gleaming white teeth and captivating me and my crew with her alluring smile.

"Have you ever acted?"

"No, Mister Wiseman," she said in a near whisper, almost as if she was divulging a secret, "but I have been in the biz for a number of years. I started out as a show girl and performed at a nightclub or two." She was acting cute and charming me with her innocence. "I did become rather well known."

In my mind's eye I could imagine her emerging from a smoke-filled speakeasy and illuminating the entire sordid surroundings like a beacon of light. Her femininity and charm were obvious, though I had the feeling she was pouring it on heavily for this audition. I explained the story line for the upcoming blockbuster movie, and she seemed more than willing to learn the part. I instructed the stage director to give her various cues and have her strike different poses. She was a quick study and followed everything to a T. The role of an Arabian queen was tailor-made for her. The decision was made then and there to cast her in the lead role. She would certainly cooperate more than some hotsy-totsy diva.

I approached Tillie, for she really had my heart pumping and I felt an indescribable attraction to this new doll. I was careful to mind my manners and not give the appearance of coming on to her too strongly. This was considered a rarity in my line of work due to the fact that most studio heads of the era would take shameful advantage of anyone and everyone. Tillie brought out the best in me and I did everything to convince her not to change her mind about working for me and, most of all, starring in our mammoth production.

With a gentlemanly smile, I asked, "You wouldn't happen to be free for the evening, Miss Thompson? I would consider it a great honor to have you join me for dinner."

Tillie was more than agreeable. Slightly blushing, she replied, "Oh, dear sir, that is such a kind offer. I'd be thrilled."

Shaking my head, I proclaimed, "Quite the contrary, my dear. The thrill is all mine."

"That it is, sir; that it is!" She winked at me.

"Would it be too presumptuous to ask where you are staying, my dear?"

Waving in a throwaway manner, Tillie answered, "Oh, over at *Hollywood Stars Hotel* on Cahuenga. I room with two other girls there."

"Does seven o'clock suit you? That should give you enough time to relax, get dressed and be ready for me, right?"

"Oooh," she peeped, "seven-ish is simple delightful." She had never poured on the charm so thick, nor had she ever spoken so carefully and correctly in her entire life.

"Fine, then. My limousine will come for you at seven on the dot. I'll let the maître d' at *The Starlight Roof* know that I wish to book a special table with a fabulous view of the city to enhance our dining pleasure."

Tillie was about to respond with something like, *"That sounds like a real fancy-schmantzy joint,"* but she hesitated and simply said, "Ooh, I'm looking so forward to having dinner with such a fine gentleman like you."

"The feeling is mutual, Tillie." I felt like a schoolboy, I was so excited. I was impressed with her speech and level of sophistication. (Boy, was I ever in for a huge shock!)

As was agreed, the studio head's chauffeur was prompt and Tillie climbed into the limo at exactly seven o'clock. She was whisked to *The Starlight Roof* and escorted by the maître d' to a secluded table at the far end of the dining room where a huge picture window opened up on the lights of Hollywood below. I stood politely as Tillie was seated. Reaching out, I held her hand gently.

"It's so nice to see you here," I said. "It seems like an eternity that we've been apart, yet it's only been a couple of hours." I could not help staring intently at her and had to avert my eyes to avoid a lustful look. I didn't want her to get any weird ideas, though I supposed she was accustomed to such things, being such a beautiful woman. Fumbling for words, I managed to stammer, "Would you care for a cocktail? They can serve us discreetly here, you know."

Tillie nodded. "I don't mind if I do," she replied. "Whatever you're having is fine with me. I'm not fussy. You know, now that you mention it, I could use a good stiff drink at the moment."

I ordered champagne for this special first occasion in Tillie's company. As the waiter poured, Tillie's eyes widened with glee. "Wow," she exclaimed, "bubbly, huh? I ain't had none o' that for a while now." Both the waiter and I were taken aback at Tillie's coarse jesting. Ignoring the obvious, I proceeded to drink a toast to my latest find.

Clinking glasses with her, I stated, "Here's to my studio's greatest and brightest new star, Tillie Thompson." She looked ravishing. "In all honesty, I must tell you that something special radiates from you, my dear woman. Just seeing you here and being alone in your presence is capturing my soul and spirit."

Tillie ate all these compliments up, and I continued to pour them on. "I admit that if someone like me can fall head over heels for you, I know the movie-going public will, too. You'll have them standing in line for a glimpse of you on the screen."

Tillie blushed ever so slightly, and it was detectable even in the dim light of the *Starlight Roof*. "Ooh," she cooed, "tell me more. You have my complete attention, and my heart is all a-flutter." She had never played the role of coquette so convincingly.

"I have big plans for you, my dear," I assured her. "Hollywood is not soon to forget the likes of Tillie." I called the waiter and ordered our meal after ascertaining what Tillie's pleasure was --- the trout almondine. I built our entire order around her choice, even though I wanted a nice big juicy, fattening steak while Tillie was careful to watch her perfect figure and request something light. We chatted amicably until the food was brought in courses. I could not take my eyes off her, and the candlelight gave her a hypnotic effect. We ate with relish and enjoyed one another's company to the fullest.

After a while our waiter handed me a shorter menu with a list of dessert offerings. "Do you still have room for a little something, Tillie? Maybe a small pudding or a thin slice of cake?"

I almost fell off my chair when she smiled and replied, "Oh, just a little something." Pausing for effect, she added, "Baked Alaska sounds scrumptious. I ain't never had it before."

Smiling, I exclaimed, "Ah, I like your style, Tillie --- a woman who lives dangerously. I'll live dangerously myself and order a chocolate mousse pie with a heavy dollop of fresh whipping cream. We can top it off with two *demitasse* orders of espresso."

Devouring our desserts and drinking our coffee gingerly, Tillie proclaimed, "This was simply divine, Mister Wiseman."

"As divine as you are, Tillie." I perceived that she could not resist my fawning over her and the compliments I continued to send her way. She wanted to hear more and more. This first evening went so well. Tillie and I became so comfortable with each other. The hours flew by quickly, and we both agreed we'd had oodles of fun.

"How about a nightcap, my dear?" I asked as we climbed into my limousine.

Shaking her head, she said, "Nuh-uh, I don't think so. Your queen of the rubies needs her beauty sleep, you know."

"Beauty sleep?" I feigned surprise. "Surely you're pulling my leg, dear. You already have natural beauty which will translate perfectly onto the screen."

Tillie giggled. "I'll bet you tell that t' all the boys --- oops, I mean, girls!" Tillie had heard rumors about certain studio bigwigs and how they didn't differentiate. "I must be kind o' *schnockered* from all that champagne!"

"Right you are, my lotus blossom," I said magnanimously. "And you are a wild one at that!" I decided to drop her at her hotel instead of taking her back to my place, a move for which she seemed grateful. "Please be ready for a studio car to pick you up at 5:30 tomorrow morning. We start at six o'clock sharp."

"Wowee!" Tillie cried. "I guess here in Hollywood the early bird really catches the worm."

"I and the crew will want you to be bright-eyed and bushy-tailed for your first day of shooting. The costume and makeup department will be working on you first, then we begin the real moviemaking process after that." Waving to her and blowing a kiss, I added, "See you in the morning!"

The next morning at five thirty the studio car rolled up in front of Tillie's hotel, and miraculously she was ready. The call had barely come to her room from the front desk when she rushed downstairs to meet the day. Muttering to herself, she said, "Jeesh, at this hour I barely had a chance t' look at myself in the mirror. I hope to hell my hair ain't ratty." She waved at the driver and they sped off. As the tires screeched on the pavement of Hollywood's deserted streets, her mind was racing. "I wonder how my first day in Tinseltown's gonna turn out. This is your big break, girl, make it a good one! This ain't no time to louse things up." Her stomach was flipping and flopping, and her nervousness was perceptible.

The workers in the costume department were busy as they ushered her anxiously in. An effeminate man with pursed lips looked her over from top to bottom and lisped, "Hmm, you'll do, dearie."

Another excited, mincing young man stepped up and practically devoured Tillie. "You must be the new hire for the lead role in *Queen of the Rubies*." Tillie nodded, trying to hold back a laugh.

"That's right, bub," she quipped. "Tillie Thompson, at yer service."

The first man sniffed disapprovingly. "You're a mess, dearie. We'll have to get right to work. A makeover will do wonders." He flicked his wrist in an alluring manner. "Once we get through with you, the movie-going public will be groveling at your feet, my sweet."

The younger man's eyes opened wide. "You'll just go bananas over the luscious men who'll be with you in the scenes they plan to shoot today. Those rippling muscles of theirs get me in a tizzy." Reflecting for a minute, obviously lost in his own fantasies regarding the macho bit players, he added, "Promise me you won't be too much of a tease, honey child."

Jokingly, Tillie replied, "I'll handle 'em with kid gloves, sweetie." She liked these two sassy boys and felt a certain camaraderie with them. "I'll wager you know just how to handle yer men, don'tcha, cutie? Don't get any hot ideas about scoring any new boyfriends. They look like they'd beat you within an inch of yer life if you so much as look at 'em the wrong way. Leave the seduction t' me, lover. I'll have 'em eatin' outta my hand before the day is over."

Pouting, the delicate older man retorted, "My, but aren't we the selfish one today! By the way, Tillie Thompson, my name is Tyler and," pointing to his partner in crime, "and this is Desmond. Pleased t' meet you. We'll be working together practically every day on this monumental turkey."

Tillie smiled sweetly. "Charmed, I'm sure." Both young men moved her through the various stages of the costuming process, and the transformation was magical.

An admiring stagehand also fluttered around her, sending loads of compliments Tillie's way and inflating her characteristically huge ego. Tyler fitted her with an ornate robe. "You'll just love this garb," he squealed. "Any queen would just die to wear what you're putting on for this role. It's covered with real diamonds and rubies, you know."

Tillie luxuriated in the softness of the velvety fabric. The train was over three feet long so that Tyler and Desmond as well as the stagehand had to lift it as she walked toward the sound stage. A throne covered in sapphire stones was prepared for the actress-queen to sit atop. The arm- and head-rests were trimmed in gold and encrusted with shiny stars. The wardrobe and makeup department personnel were pleased beyond belief at Tillie's stunning appearance.

"Absolutely splendid, my dear," Tyler gushed. "I shall bow to my queen."

Tillie chuckled. "Ain'tcha mistaken, Hon? In yer case it'd be a curtsey!"

Desmond stepped in and scolded, "Now, now! You're being a nasty queeny-weeny, Your Highness!"

"Queeny-weeny?" Tillie shot back. "Whadya

speakin', Pig Latin or somethin'? Yer in th' presence of yer queen, you knave. Bow to me, or I'll chop off yer head!"

Tyler covered his mouth and giggled. "I can only guess which head you mean, Your Majesty!" He escorted her over to Johnny, the makeup specialist who did a last minute touchup on her. He had a more serious mien than the wardrobe boys. He sniffed disapprovingly and couldn't hold back his sarcasm.

"*Queen of the Rubies*, indeed," he grunted. "Another potboiler from this travesty that passes for a motion picture studio." Glancing at Tillie and shaking his head in dismay, he added, "So you're supposed to be the queen, huh? You look more like a warmed-over, rundown version of the Bride of Frankenstein. Knowing this joint, they'll probably make a movie out o' that one of these days, too. It'll either be a winner or a big flop."

Tillie became huffy. "At least I'm more of a queen than you'll ever be. And a real one at that, Twinkle-Toes! Why, just look at this fabulous robe. Bet yer jealous as all gittup!"

"Ha!" Johnny cried. "It's the face that makes it on the screen, you amateur, not the robe." Preparing to get to work at once, he added, "Now, my so-called queen, please do me the courtesy of remaining seated so that I can perform my job on you properly."

"On this crummy chair?" Tillie snapped.

"Well, what did you expect, dearie? Something with a glittery star on it? It's a makeup chair and it'll do for the likes of someone like you. As the saying went in olden times, 'sit your royal tush down right here!' First, we've got to get rid of all this goop on your face --- it's simply atrocious."

Tillie rolled her eyes in disgust. "Oh yeah? Listen, Bub, I'll have you know this 'goop' is the best money can buy. Nothin' but the best for me, you know."

"The way it looks on you, sweetie," Johnny retorted, "I'd ask for my money back. Now then, please sit still and stop your squirming. The makeup I'm using here will prepare you for today's shooting. Believe me, it'll be a major undertaking."

Tillie quieted down and sat through the entire process obediently. After a while she became impatient and fidgety. "Ain't you done yet, Mac?" she snarled. "You keep me sittin' here for over an hour and yer still not through, for cryin' out loud."

Johnny barked back at her. "Listen here, queen bee, don't get your stinger out o' joint. Settle down. We're almost through. And Heaven knows I can hardly wait 'til this is all over."

Another half hour went by. Johnny stood back, looked at his creation and exclaimed, "Well, miracle of miracles --- it's finished." Handing her a mirror, he said encouragingly, "Take a gander at your new kisser."

Tillie glanced and her eyes widened in amazement. "Golly," she cried, "that ain't me, is it?

Why, I don't recognize myself. I sat for a long time and I ended up with *this*?"

Johnny shot her a look of contempt. "What's wrong now, Miss Prima Donna?"

"Listen here, Mister," she growled, "I was gonna give you a bunch o' compliments, but you made me look like crap."

Pitching his nose in the air, Johnny responded angrily, "Too bad, Miss Know-it-all. Take it, leave it or lump it, for all I care. I'm throwin' in the friggin' towel. I doesn't matter to me if you're the ever lovin' Queen of Sheba. Do me a favor and get lost." Both Johnny and Tillie stormed out in opposite directions, crossing the sound stage in a rage.

Folding her arms in defiance, she yelled, "I'm the queen and I'll have that crumb-bum's head on a platter!" The crew was stunned, then broke out in applause for Tillie's marvelous dramatic acting skills. She curtseyed shyly and blushed.

Entering the set where the initial filming was to take place, Tillie noticed a director seated in a canvas-back chair, surrounded by an entire crew of various personnel. The atmosphere was electric even at this early hour of the morning.

"We've been expecting you, my dear," the director said, standing respectfully and speaking in a cheerful manner. "You look ravishing, like a queen indeed. Let's get right to work, shall we?" He resumed his seat and grabbed a huge megaphone to shout orders to his crew.

Tillie was led to the throne placed in the center of the ornately decorated set. A pair of near-naked bit players acting as guards entered. "Let's have you stand on either side of our star, please," the director said politely. Looking around, he snapped his fingers and, temper flaring, yelled, "Where in blazes is that damn prop man? Man, they've saddled me with a bunch of no-count bums. Can't seem to get any good help these days."

A hapless, shabby-looking man walked slowly up to the director. "Yes, sir?" he asked meekly.

"Run and grab me a pair of ostrich-feather fans from shelf seventeen," the director barked. It only took a couple of minutes for the raggedy man to run back and forth with the requested items. Waving them wildly, he inadvertently tripped and fell. The fans flew out of his hands and landed directly in front Tillie as she sat on the throne. The prop man picked himself up, bowed before Tillie and scooped up the feather fans.

"Pray tell," he asked, "to whom should I give these feathery contraptions?"

The director was steaming mad and shouted, "Who do you think, you idiot? Give them to the President of the United States." The prop man looked more confused than ever until the director added, a bit more gently, "To the guards standing on either side of our queen, if you would be so kind. I can safely say that if you had a brain you might become dangerous."

"Look on the bright side, sir," the prop man responded, smiling brightly. "If I have no brain, I really can't do much harm now, can I?"

The director shook his head and chuckled to himself. "Where on God's green Earth did we ever find this winner?" he muttered. Taking up his duties as director once again, he shouted through the megaphone, "Would the guards please begin fanning your queen slowly and seductively?"

Tillie was distracted by the two muscular actors playing the obedient guards. She devoured every inch of their flesh with her huge eyes. The director noticed her level of attention. He needed to refocus her and have her concentrate on the scene at hand. "Now, Tillie, please envision yourself as the mighty queen, giving orders to your faithful servants. Instruct them to leave your presence and go instead to the caves where the precious diamonds and rubies of your realm are stored. Order them to guard this treasure with their very lives!"

Tillie went into action, gesturing in a commanding way and mouthing the words of a royal edict. Her facial expressions, the way she used her fingers and hands plus the heightened emotion she felt impressed even the seasoned director. He began to realize how gifted this young "amateur" could be.

The queen's "guards" bowed to her and went off to do Tillie's bidding. The director was satisfied with the scene and yelled, "Cut! Print!" Getting up from his chair and rushing over to her, he clasped her hands warmly and exclaimed, "That was marvelous, my dear, simply divine. Rarely have I ever seen anyone take my direction with such perfect execution. I can see that you're going to bring excitement to the screen." He directed his stage manager to announce the lunch break. "We'll return at one o'clock sharp to film a few more scenes."

I met Tillie outside the studio and together we walked across the street to *Sam's Deli*. We sat and chatted about the first day of filming. Tillie was all jazzed when I said, "The director tells me you're doing a bang-up job."

With her usual nonchalance, Tillie replied, "Nothin' to it, really --- piece o' cake. I've got 'em groveling at my feet. I *am* the Queen, of course!"

I smiled and said, "You exhibit great charm, confidence and beauty, my dear. I just love the way you speak to me." I didn't want to beat around the bush and asked, "By the way, are you free this evening? I'd love to invite you to my little hideaway up in the hills overlooking Hollywood."

Blushing slightly, Tillie chirped, "Rather forward of ya, don'tcha think?" Before I had a chance to catch my breath, she quickly added, "You know I'd love it! The Queen is used to commanding her subjects, but in your case I'll obey and am willing to, how shall I say, *perform* for you alone."

Mesmerized by her brash manner, I asserted, "No doubt you will, my sweet. You're such a little tease!"

"I'll be more than that after I finish with you

tonight, Mister," she purred.

"Promise, my love?"

"You gotta know by now that I never break my word."

The waiter took our order: Tillie's Reuben with a dollop of the joint's special Russian dressing, while I chose the open-face chopped liver and pastrami special with a Kosher pickle on the side. We ate with gusto and continued chatting, almost playfully. Our talk got around to the sensitive subject of her contract. She was excited to hear about her take in the deal.

"The initial contract has a two-year duration, Tillie," I explained. "You'll be earning five hundred a week to start. Raises will follow and I think you'll be pleased. I have papers ready for you to sign, if you care to come to my office after today's shooting winds down."

Tillie nodded affirmatively several times during the remainder of our lunch. We continued to munch away on our sandwiches, smiling at one another.

The rest of the day went very well for Tillie. "We should be able to finish ahead of schedule," the director said at one point, "even a month earlier." He expressed how proud he was of her. "It is customary to have a premiere screening when the film is completed. All the bigshots from Hollywood and a boatload of critics attend. We're keeping our fingers crossed for *Queen of the Rubies* to be our biggest hit yet."

Tillie rubbed her knuckles against her breast and wistfully blew at them. "With me as your queen," she quipped, "it'll be a cinch. I'll knock 'em dead." Her penchant for bragging and showing off hadn't subsided since her arrival in Tinseltown. Truly, her ego knew no limits.

At the end of the day she strolled over to my office. My secretary received her in the lobby prior to my return.

"My boss wants you to look over these papers before he gets back," the secretary said, handing Tillie the contract which had been drawn up. "If you have questions, you'll be able to ask him right away because you'll know what's in it."

Tillie was all smiles when she entered after being summoned. She forced me to smile ear from ear, too. "Step right into my office," I said, taking off my coat and offering her a seat.

"Thanks," she responded, "my dogs're killin' me after a long day o' shootin' and I need t' take the load off." She proceeded to give me a blow-by-blow account of her day at the studio, even going over things we'd discussed previously at lunch. I directed her attention back to the contract and answered all her questions, most of which were about money. Then I instructed my secretary to inform the chauffeur that my car should be brought around. I wanted to get Tillie up to my place as quickly as possible. We made ourselves comfortable in the back of the limo. It was the beginning of a sizzling romantic evening.

Jenkins, my butler, greeted us warmly when we arrived home. I ordered him to procure a special bottle of wine from the cellar and serve it out in the rose garden. Holding hands with Tillie, I sat her down on one of the plush chairs arranged around the ornate tea table. We enjoyed the wine immensely, drinking glass after glass, probably imbibing more than we could safely handle.

As the evening wore on, we eventually left the rose garden and wandered upstairs, reaching my bedroom. The woozy feeling from the wine gave us light heads. We made wild, passionate love for hours, humping away like jack rabbits. Such arousal and merry lovemaking had seldom been seen by the world's mortals.

A month had passed, the film was in the can, so to speak, and ready for the premiere showing. The renowned *Emerald Palace Theatre* was the scene of the gala sendoff for *Queen of the Rubies*. It was a more than appropriate venue for the first showing of such a film. The studio's decorators were able to utilize features of the theatre's interior to heighten the excitement. Huge floodlights dominated the Hollywood sky, and the red carpet had been rolled out to receive a contingent of the town's biggest and brightest luminaries. Tillie's name and the title of the movie flashed in lights on the huge marquee and could be seen for blocks up and down Hollywood Boulevard.

A huge red carpet was laid out. Newspaper reporters and columnists streamed in and plied the celebrities with questions for their readers, satisfying everyone's intrigue about the glamorous lives of movie stars. Each reporter felt his or her scoop was bigger and better than the nearest competition.

Upon our arrival (I say "our" because Tillie clung tightly to me as the cameras flashed wildly, almost blinding us both), we tried to make our way through the dense crowd of onlookers and admirers. The fans' arms were stretched out and their hands tried to touch Tillie's splendid dress which was just out of reach. A few of the onlookers sought to shake my own hand, too. The applause and cheers were deafening, especially the joyous chanting of "Till-lee, Till-lee" over and over without end. She waved back and strutted her stuff provocatively, so to speak.

It took us several minutes to get through all the mayhem in the front of the theatre and make it into the lobby for more snapping of pictures and popping of flashbulbs. An usher escorted us to our seats, and I had to hand it to them for the efficient way they took care of everything that night. I looked around and picked out various faces from the crowd: members of the cast, personnel from the crew and studio bigwigs who had made this mega-production possible. Tillie looked around just as avidly, turning around and taking special note of Johnny, the makeup specialist seated a few rows in back of us. Under her breath I heard her mutter, "Oh God, I think I'm gonna have a gas attack. I wish I could blow a nice smelly one his way and really knock him out."

Her musings didn't surprise me in the least. After all, Tillie hadn't changed from one day to the next; she was merely being herself, the inimitable Tillie. The assembled crowd quieted down, and that was my cue to walk onto the stage to deliver a short address.

"Good evening, ladies and gentlemen," I began, "and thank you all for coming out tonight to view our multimillion dollar extravaganza, *Queen of the Rubies*. Without further ado, here's our motion picture which I hope you'll enjoy and tell everybody about."

The lights dimmed, the curtain pulled back to reveal the screen. Running time was one hour and fifteen minutes, after which thunderous applause filled the cinema's auditorium. Cheers of "More, more!" and "Encore, encore!" echoed through the vast hall. Turning to Tillie I gave her a hug and a kiss.

"Well, well, my queen," I said jovially, "it appears that this film will be a huge success." The proof of my statement was in the pudding: tallies of ticket sales a couple of weeks later exceeded my expectations with the highest earnings for a single motion picture ever put out by our studio.

Such a positive audience reaction was highly unusual. *Variety*, the trade publication which was always on the cutting edge of everything coming out of Hollywood, printed the words, "BOX OFFICE

SMASH, QUEEN OF RUBIES BREAKS ALL RECORDS," on their front page. I envisioned other big pictures in store for Tillie: *The Spy Girl* and *A Lady's Delight*. I had read the scripts and felt that Tillie was perfect for the lead roles in both productions. Visions of dancing dollar signs spun around in my head. Tillie was a dream-come-true for me as well as the studio's pocketbook.

Tillie used my car and my personal chauffeur for a night out on the town. Heaven only knew where she was going; she had turned into such a flighty little thing. Taking off in haste, Tillie leaned over to instruct my cooperative and complicit chauffeur, "Hey, Bub, point this tub in the direction o' that new club on the Sunset Strip I heard about, *The Golden Zebra*. Sounds like a schnazzy joint and I wanna perk things up a bit."

Pulling up in front of the nightclub's entrance, a doorman helped her out of the limo. He and the chauffeur exchanged knowing looks. Golden lights illuminated the huge statue of a zebra, flickering for all passing by on the boulevard to see and admire. Tillie heard music blasting from inside the club. "Man, that sounds like a jivey beat, somethin' I could get my tootsies movin' to and my body shakin' up a storm."

Tillie was greeted by a good-looking dark haired man dressed in a tuxedo. He led her to a choice table within an earshot of the swinging orchestra. She couldn't take her eyes off the man who had accompanied her. A pert waitress holding a serving tray stepped up and asked saucily, "What's yer pleasure, Honey?"

Tillie winked and replied, "Well, for starters I'll take that hunk who was at my side the minute I stepped into this joint." Pausing for effect, she added, "But to be more realistic, I'd like a glass o' Beefeaters Gin, straight up, no ice."

The band began playing some of the current greatest hits: *Some of these Days*, *My Blue Heaven* and *Can't Help Lovin' Dat Man*, to name a few. The dance floor filled with patrons anxious to shake their tootsies and trip the light fantastic.

Tillie sipped her gin and glanced around. "This is *my* kind o' place, for sure," she told herself, "really swingin'." All the male patrons were dressed to the nines, but one in particular caught her eye for the elegance and certain amount of brash confidence he exuded. Her attention instantly focused on him as others faded in the background. Her mind was reeling.

"Wow," she bristled, "that's one fine lookin' dude. I'd love to play Spanky-Cakes with *him*." The guy was aware of Tillie's fixated gaze and flashed her a winning smile. Tillie's knees grew weak and her heart was all aflutter. At one point the guy consulted with the hostess, and soon Tillie found a fresh glass of gin placed before her.

"That gentleman over there," she whispered to Tillie and gesturing toward the man, "wants to know if you'll do him the pleasure of your company." Before she finished saying the words, the guy had crossed the room and was at Tillie's table.

"Good evening there, my fine young lady," he said, bowing slightly. "And you certainly are a fine one at that."

Tillie blushed and batted her eyelashes. "Why, thank you, Mister....?"

"Harkin --- Tom Harkin. You won't mind if I join you?"

Nodding, Tillie gushed, "Oh no, for sure. Sit yer fanny right down."

Taking the chair opposite Tillie and surveying his surroundings, he remarked "This joint's one of my favorite hangouts. I come here all the time. What about you?"

Tillie stared at him and answered, "This is my first time. I can tell already that I'm gonna like it here. The atmosphere is swingin'."

"So whad're we sittin' here for like two bumps on the log?" Tom blurted. "Let's hit that dance floor, Sugar Lips."

Tillie stood and practically melted into Tom Harkin's arms as he lavished attention on her. "I love cuttin' a rug with you, Hon," she quipped. After a lively foxtrot, the band switched to a Charleston, and then a slow, romantic dance with one of the big hits of the day, *Someone to Watch Over Me*.

The two were drawn to one another, and their hormones raged like teenagers. Every chance they got they necked while seated at the table as smoke from the club's patrons swirled around them. Tillie felt as if this new stranger was taking her life over. Her attraction for the wild side was fulfilled in him. Something wilder was surely coming her way and she bit off more than she could chew.

For this "elegant" stranger was in reality a chiseling, raggedy-ass conman. He specialized in gambling, swindling and pimping. He was capable of razzle-dazzling the skirt off any woman. The innocent, naïve ones were more susceptible to his charms. He raked in money from his gambling and prostitution rings. I wished I would have known with whom she was cheating on me so that I could have warned her. She hid it from me, however, and I remained totally unaware of her involvement.

They ended up at Tom Harkin's place and made love the entire night. It was the beginning of an extremely hot romance, one that she was barely able to handle. She slipped away from Tom and stumbled back to my place close to six o'clock in the morning. Of course I had stayed awake, worried to death and confronted her when she came in.

"Where have you been, Tillie?" I asked, hiding my anger and disillusion. She careened past me, trying to ignore me with a devil-may-care gesture. Turning abruptly, she flashed me a look of contempt.

"What's it to ya?" she snarled. "I was nursing a sick girlfriend I used to room with back at the hotel. I sat up with her all night, if ya really wanna know.

Now I'm tired, so leave me the hell alone, will ya?"

I confronted her with kid gloves. "Would you try to remember that it is important for me to know where you are at all times?" I asked. "After all, we are living together. It's the only fitting and proper thing to do, considering…." Noting how she blankly stared at me, I added, "When you show up in this condition, it makes me wonder about you. Besides, there's important business I need to go over concerning your next movie."

Tillie furrowed her brow. "Business?" she cried. "Is that all you think about: business and your damn moolah? I'm more than that, Buster, and don't you forget it! Without me you're nothin'. Them movies you churn out from that shithole of a studio are zilch. I'm your real bread 'n butter, your meal ticket." Looking around and sniffing, she added, "By the way, I'm starvin' t' death. Where the hell is my breakfast?"

I was bowled over by the way she marched in and started giving orders to the staff. "Get that sorry excuse for a cook out here on the double," she barked. When the frightened man stepped in, she got right in his face and yelled, "Fix me two eggs over easy plus a bagel and cream cheese, Luigi or whatever your name is. And don't forget a pot of strong coffee and a tall glass of fresh-squeezed orange juice either. And them eggs better not be runny like the last time, *paisan*!" She was making fun of the hapless man's nationality.

I couldn't stand her treatment of my trusted staff

and scolded her for her brashness. She appeared to ignore me, letting my sharp words go in one ear and out the other. Her poisonous look was all I could bear and I cowered in embarrassment.

"If he can't take the heat," she growled, "he'd better get outta that damn kitchen. Fire the damn wops's ass, for all I care!" Pushing me aside, she said snipingly, "I gotta wash up for breakfast. You ain't got no problems with that, do ya?"

Sitting at table, she became impatient all over again. "Hey," she shouted, "where's my grub? Can't you see this dame is starvin'?" The beaten-down cook handed the tray to the servant and it was presented to Tillie. She took a few bites and winced.

"Cold, dammit," she screeched. "The damn food's cold. I ain't got no appetite no more." Turning to me as I watched in horror, she asked, "Where'd ya get these bums? Ain't there no good help around here in Hollywood these days?"

Casting all my disillusion aside, I insisted that we go over the details of the new movie in which she would star. Tillie was out of hand and I couldn't figure out what was troubling her.

As the morning rolled on I finally was able to convince her to settle down. We chatted and discussed the topic which interested her the most: her upcoming movie role in *Spy Girl*. Her mind seemed to be elsewhere, though. When the evening rolled around, Tillie readied herself to go out again. Giving me a quick peck on the cheek, she breezed off. I didn't utter a word and was appalled that she didn't give a damn about me or our relationship.

"That ungrateful dame!" I muttered to myself. "I'll probably have to do a bit of snooping on my own." I consulted with my chauffeur and he agreed to provide the lowdown on what I needed to know. I asked him first where he had dropped Tillie off the previous night and how long she had stayed.

"I dunno, sir," the man replied. "Miss Tillie never called for me to pick her back up once I returned here."

Rubbing my chin and thinking, I said, "She got back here somehow. Did you happen to see who brought her back?"

"One of the maids told me about seeing her step from a shiny black limo parked just outside the main gate, sir." The chauffeur blushed slightly and bowed his head. "It is only hearsay, though, since I didn't see her myself."

I pondered those observations and figured out that someone else was involved in her life, hence she was no longer so lovey-dovey with me anymore. I suspected this would happen sooner or later. That broad doesn't seem to have a soul.

Tillie drove the roadster I'd lent her directly to the *Golden Zebra Club* again that night. Tom Harkin was right there to meet her. She raced into his arms, unashamedly. Another evening of drinking, dancing, cavorting and necking in public ensued. Late night had them once again flitting off in Harkin's car and spending time together making wild passionate love on the couch, loveseat, a second divan and eventually the huge bed in the man's spacious penthouse.

Lying next to one another and smoking cigarettes after a particularly frisky session, Tillie's natural curiosity awakened. "Say, lover," she asked, "you never told me what ya did for a livin', y'know."

Snuffing out his cig and pulling her closer to him, he whispered, "Don'tcha know? I'm a jack-of-all-trades, babe."

"Hmm," she purred, "just what sorts o' trades, if it ain't too personal?"

"Oh," he answered nonchalantly, "just businesses in general. For instance, the ponies."

"I'm wild about horses, lover," Tillie squealed. "Even placed a bet or two in my time."

Harkin perked up. "Just my type o' dame. I can give ya pointers on how to do it the right way."

Nudging his cheek and then planting a huge kiss on his lips, she cooed, "You can give me pointers on anything you want, Mister. For starters you can spread these legs o' mine again and point that big hunk o' flesh ya got right at me."

Tillie may have thought brighter days were ahead for her, but little did she suspect she was treading on some dangerous territory. She was playing with fire and about to get burned very severely.

They both shacked up regularly and engaged in much pillow talk. At one point Harkin asked Tillie what she did for a living. "You're so mysterious, my dear," he exclaimed, "and I feel I don't know you at all."

Tillie smirked and replied, "Oh, I've been around, doin' the things a flapper normally does. Y'know, stuff like singin' and dancin' in a whole bunch o' flea-bitten joints which they have the nerve t' call nightclubs. One bum offered me a measly three-year contract. Why, that's like a crummy piss in a paper cup. Another jerk, the owner of a fly-by-night record company, had me do a few sides."

Tillie's unique way of expressing herself really turned Harkin on, and he groped her without stopping as she spoke, ruffling all the bed covers. She squirmed with delight.

"By the way," he put it, "you ain't gonna tell me you fell in love with any o' them other guys, are ya?"

"Nuh-uh," she answered with a frown. "In the end all they wanted was t' get in a girl's panties."

"I s'ppose that means you ain't wit' anybody now, right?"

"Uhm," she began, "there's this one guy who owns a movie production company. He saw my talent and cast me in some role. It came out in the flickers a couple weeks back. It's called *Queen of the Rubies*. The clunker actually made a li'l bit o' bread for me and the studio, wouldn't ya know. It ain't no wonder the guy likes me so much. Wiseman a two-bit oversexed horny toad, if ya ask me. We've slept together and he's got it in that head of his that we're some kind o' item." Cuddling up closer to Harkin, she added, "What I really need is a man who can show a girl some real action, y'know. Somethin' to really turn me on. The thought of you, f'r instance, arouses the blazes outta me. For you I'd spread 'em morning, noon and night."

Harkin rubbed his chin and said, "Oh, yeah. I've heard o' Wiseman. The guy's known for pickin' up dames and usin' 'em for one o' his money-makin' enterprises."

Tillie nodded. "It figures," she replied, groaning. "One o' the first things he did was grab my hot box, y'know. Kind of a grand opening, awfully quick, though."

Harkin drew her closer and asserted, "Well, I can see his point. But he ain't got half the adventure in 'im like I got. Why don't ya join me and we can cook up a few wild times together?"

"Tell me more," Tillie exclaimed. "But we ain't gonna say another word until you and me take another roll in the hay."

After prolonged lovemaking and a cigarette or two more smoked down to the stubs, Harkin asked Tillie, "I take it you'll be free this weekend, Babe."

"You betcha, Lover Boy. Whadya got in mind?"

"Just thought it'd be a nice idea to drive you out to the races. You can get a load o' what I do out there."

"You got yerself a deal, Mac."

Harkin held her tight and proclaimed, "Tillie, I'm

crazy 'bout ya and wanna make all your dreams come true."

Dawn came earlier than both of them expected. Tom offered Tillie breakfast. She ate hers quickly, then took advantage of his kindness in running her back to Wiseman's mansion. He scrawled his name and phone number on the inside of a matchbox cover from *The Golden Zebra*. "Don't forget to ring me up," he said in a commanding way.

Tillie slinked up to the entrance of the mansion, then collected her wits and knocked. She greeted Wiseman's butler and strolled in merrily. Her benefactor was dressed and ready to head out to the studio.

"Morning, Tillie," he said fleetingly. "See you later, my dear." Turning around abruptly, he decided to give her (and himself) the shadow of a doubt and kissed her on the cheek. Tillie forced herself not to pull away, almost as if negative poles of a magnet were rubbing together.

She spent the remainder of the day preparing for her next starring role. "*Spy Girl* my eye!" she sniffed, reflecting bitterly about a film she was sure would flop at the box office. During a break in reading the script she removed the matchbox cover from her pocketbook and turned it over between her fingers several times, finally deciding to give Harkin a call. She wasn't even concentrating on the script anymore, but allowed her mind to be flooded with thoughts of Tom Harkin and him alone.

Dialing the number, she noticed that the connection had barely been made and the phone scarcely registered a full ring before Harkin's voice came over the line like gangbusters. "What's cookin', Doll?" he cooed.

Tillie was amazed. "How'd ya know it was me callin'? Anyhow, I'm takin' ya up on yer offer and wanna see ya again tonight."

"I'll be there at seven t' get ya," Harkin shot back. "Be ready for some hot action."

Forgetting the script and throwing it off to one side, she ran upstairs to bathe, get dressed and array herself like never before for her new lover.

Harkin had the night all planned out, whisking the ravishing Tillie off to *The Ace is Wild* club located up in a deserted cul-de-sac in the Hollywood Hills. A parking attendant took charge of Harkin's sedan car and the two went inside after giving the secret knock and waiting for a countersign from the host. Tillie was amazed at the atmosphere, since the "club" looked like nothing from the outside. The space was divided into several rooms. The booze flowed freely, the air was full of cigarette smoke and a sultry blond in a sparkly evening dress crooned a popular tune to the accompaniment of a small orchestra. Tillie reflected for a minute or two about the days when she had started out singing in clubs herself. Harkin shook her out of her daydreams.

"Time to play, kitten," he managed to say to her over the noise. They headed to a door at the far end of a hallway. Rapping on it with a series of knocks, it opened and the two went inside. Gambling tables were set up in a large salon. The host greeted Harkin warmly, and he was unmistakably impressed with Tillie's appearance.

"And who is this delightful creature?" the tuxedoed man asked.

"That's Tillie. I've been hidin' her away."

"Wowee! She's some sexy babe!"

Harkin grabbed the man by the collar and snarled, "Have a little respect for the lady, Buster. She's high class, not like the rabble ya usually have struttin' 'round this joint." In a huff Harkin turned to Tillie and escorted her to the gambling tables, giving her the grand tour of the various games going on. She became particularly fascinated with roulette.

"Can ya buy me some chips, Hon?" she asked. "I'd like t' place a bet. I'm feelin' lucky, thanks t' you." She learned that betting amounts began at the staggering amount of one hundred dollars. "Place it on number 13," she suggested, in spite of that number's questionable connotations.

Once all the bets were in, the croupier spun the wheel. Lo and behold, it landed on 13. Piles of chips were pushed Tillie's way on the table. She keep those on the same number, the wheel was spun and came up on 13 several more times. Harkin advised her to take her chips off the table and move on to something else. Over five hundred dollars' worth of chips were piled up, but Tillie insisted on placing one more bet. Harkin grasped her arm, and not gently either.

"I'm orderin' ya t' scoop up yer damn chips 'n move yer butt off that chair *now*!" When she didn't show any intention to move, he yanked her off the chair and dragged her across the room. Pushing her against a wall and telling her threateningly, "Don't move an inch from this spot until I tell ya!" She waited obediently and watched how he rushed back to the roulette table to gather up the piles of chips, placing them in the pockets of his suit to the point where they bulged. He strode back in her direction carefully, grabbed her by the arm again and led her to the cashier's window.

"Take care of this for me, Wilkinson," he said commandingly to the meek man behind the bars of the cashier's window whose eyes bulged as the great quantity of chips was emptied into a sliding drawer for him to retrieve securely from inside the office. "I'll pick up the winnings before I head out tonight with this dumbbell here." He made a crude gesture toward Tillie who stuck her tongue out at him in response.

"What's the big deal?" she squealed when they got into a quiet corner and had two glasses of bourbon on the rocks handed to them by a cocktail waitress. "Can't a girl place a lousy bet without a buttinsky like you intrudin'?"

Pointing a finger at her only a few inches from her nose, he mumbled, "Every damn table in this place is fixed, you numbskull. It was rigged for ya t' lose that last bet. You can thank yer lucky stars I intervened 'n yanked ya outta there before you lost a shitload of moolah for yerself."

Tillie's face shriveled with fright. "Gosh, I'm sorry, babe," she whispered, "I had no idea. I ain't never been in a place like this before. It's my first time."

Harkin frowned. "If ya continue screwin' things up like ya have," he growled, "there ain't gonna be no second time, lamebrain. This place's a goldmine. I'm thinkin' seriously about usin' some o' my connections to take it over soon. I don't need the likes of somebody like you muckin' up the goddamn works before I get my lunch hooks on it. *Capeesh*?"

Tillie smirked and replied, "Yeah, I *capeesh*. A girl ain't even allowed t' have a l'il bit o' fun when you're around."

"If you had half a brain," he retorted, "you'd stay back at Wiseman's place 'n study yer lousy scripts. Ain't no use blowin' yer star status t' smithereens. I'm callin' a cab for ya so's you can head back there now. I ain't wastin' no more time with ya tonight. I'll look ya up again after I snag the deal on this joint. That'll give ya enough time to churn out a couple more flickers 'n make a couple thousand dollars to bring t' the tables if ya want. It don't bother me none if ya wanna throw away yer own filthy money." Leading her toward the door where they first entered, he instructed the tuxedoed host, "Make sure this dame gets back home right away. The cab's comin' t' get her *pronto*."

Tillie returned to the mansion around midnight and felt dejected. "Imagine that," she thought, "me bein' thrown ov'r by some two-bit gambler. But maybe he's right. After all, I got me a pretty good racket goin' here with them flickers. Guess I lost sight o' my God given talent t' act 'n please the penny-ante movie goers." She also reasoned that if she made enough of her own money and wanted to gamble it to win more, she wouldn't have to depend on any Tom, Dick or Harry to support her in that endeavor.

"Hiya, Snookums," she said sweetly as she climbed into my bed and cuddled with me tightly. It was the beginning of a fruitful year or two when Tillie's affection for me blossomed. Her devotion to learning her parts for the upcoming films in which she starred was unmistakable. She also dedicated much of her free time to answering her fan mail, autographing glossy photos of herself for her adoring public and appearing at a number of gala events to promote my studio and our star-studded productions like *Spy Girl*, *A Lady's Delight* and *The Vamp from Havana*.

The last picture, one which was partially filmed in the new medium of sound and which featured Tillie playing the role of Conchita, a tropical nightclub entertainer who sings and dances her way into the hearts of several admiring men amid swaying palm trees and the torrid rhythms of Alejandro Valdez and his orchestra, endeared her to the whole idea of the mysteries of Cuba. Even more vibrant was her attraction to Alejandro, a dancer named Luis, assorted band members who flashed admiring glances at her during the filming, and the whole idea of exotic lovemaking with tall, dark strangers in a land far removed from the rat race stateside.

"Just like in Caliente and all down Mexico way," Luis explained to her, "Cuban rum flows freely. You can get a buzz legally any day of the week in Havana, the sin capital of the Caribbean."

"Sin capital?" Tillie asked, surprised at the boldness she rarely heard in American men. "Whadya mean?"

"I mean, anything goes," Luis responded, grinning with glee. "And anytime you want." Making a sweeping gesture with his hand toward the studio lights and cameras, he added, "All stateside is good for is the money you can earn to take back down there and have a ball. Otherwise, it's Dullsville, *querida*."

Tillie became enthralled with the idea of sailing away with Luis, Alejandro or any of the band members and settling in sunny, humid and bawdy Havana. More speed was given to her thoughts about Cuba when her next movie came out as the Great Depression hit the public fairly hard. For the first time, Tillie flopped with her portrayal of Marie Antoinette in *Let Them Eat Cake*. It was a role that rubbed moviegoers the wrong way. It was all my fault: my production staff persuaded me to go ahead with the picture because we had too much invested in costumes, props and special technicians who had been brought in to assist. I should have put a stop to the idea of building a huge replica of the Versailles Palace on the backlot of the studio, too. I was too smitten with Tillie's affection to think straight in those days, never imagining that she had other extremely different plans and ideas while she was cuddling up to me every night.

In spite of all the ups and downs in Tillie's life, she could never shake the idea of how Tom Harkin had thrown her over after that notorious evening when they visited the *Ace in the Hole* club with its illegal casino operation in the Hollywood Hills. "I'm the only one who does the throwin' over in this town," she hissed to Alejandro Valdez after they had completed an intricate musical number for *The Vamp from Havana* talkie. "I'll get even with that bastard someday, even if it's the last thing I do before blowin' Tinseltown."

Alejandro smiled from ear to ear. "When you depart, *peloncita*," he murmured seductively, "allow me to invite you to visit me and the band in Cuba. We plan to go back after the picture is completed."

Tillie grinned and moved closer to him. "You ain't goin' nowhere," she purred. "I hear through the grapevine that Wiseman wants to keep you and your boys here for another couple of flicks. The rumba's gettin' popular here, especially now that Cugat and his orchestra are performin' every night at the

Waldorf back in New York. He plans on givin' ya a raise and some very attractive contractual terms, Honey Bun. You and your band may never wanna return to the island."

Shaking his head, Valdez exclaimed, *"No es posible*. It will never happen, my dear. We want to go back to Cuba and stay forever. Hollywood is nice, but Havana is far nicer."

These words, plus so many more overtures from Valdez, his band members, Luis the dancing fool and her role as in *The Vamp from Havana* started swaying her whole manner of thinking and making considerations for her future. She was a risk taker by nature. She intended to take her biggest risk by getting even with Harkin, so why not go all the way and steal away to magical, mysterious Cuba? The prospect sounded more alluring with each passing day.

I have to admit I became more depressed about the failure of *Let Them Eat Cake* than Tillie ever was. She seemed infallible, while I took the fall pretty hard. The big crash on Wall Street had also wiped out all my investments on the stock market, so everyone at the studio including myself was counting on having a few blockbuster hits to keep things afloat. It hurt me to have to lay folks off because the projects were few and work began lacking, but the handwriting was on the wall.

On the other hand, Tillie took things completely in stride. Gauging me as a failure, she shunned me once

again and began stepping out practically every night. I was too beside myself with grief and worry to inquire where she went and with whom. At times she would return in the wee hours of the morning, while on many other occasions she neglected to come back to my hilltop home at all.

DANGEROUS INTERLUDE WITH TOM HARKIN

Tillie was far from idle during the first few months after the "Black Tuesday Blues" had set in. Newspapers were filled with photos of mayhem on the floor of the New York Stock Exchange. Victims of the crash came in all shapes, sizes and levels of affluence. Millionaires lost just as much, maybe even more when the percentages were tallied, than the housewives, salesgirls or bellboys who had dabbled in shares. Though economic collapses had occurred many times before throughout the turbulent course of American history, this particular one had been a gradual slump which didn't reveal itself fully until October 1929. Years later, people would take a tally of the devastating effect it had on human lives. For now, there was disillusion coast to coast, and it was running deeper with each passing day.

Tillie remained abreast of all the developments via newspapers and numerous radio reports, but her attitude was largely indifferent. She knew that not everyone had been wiped out. For example, she had neither invested in the stock market nor performed all the dizzying trades on margin people her age had been doing for years. She also kept very little money in regular banks, suspecting that they couldn't be trusted to handle it. She had placed the bulk of her earnings in gilt-edge securities and municipal bonds which were much more secure and sheltered from weird fluctuations in the economy.

"That Wiseman character is a big loser," she reasoned while sipping a sherry in a private cabaña at Malibu Beach and looking out at the sun setting over the Pacific. "I gotta start spreadin' my wings and lookin' out for Number One here. And I'm sure gettin' fed up with all this Tinseltown crap floatin' around. Damn, people around here ain't got no more class than those bums back in New York. The only excitin' people I've run into so far out here are Alex, Louie and the boys from Cuba."

Tillie didn't realize it at the time, but in her mind she was already formulating plans to run far away. She did, however, have one account to settle before she hightailed it from the town she pejoratively referred to as "the Land of Fruits and Nuts." She had never shaken the humiliation of the night when Tom Harkin had gotten cross with her about the roulette setup and packed her off in a cab, brusquely ejecting her from the *Ace in the Hole Club*. Her patience was enduring, and her plans to get even with him took on a scientific brilliance in the way she organized it and intended to carry it out.

"Let's just see if his offer to invite me out to bet on the ponies still stands," she told herself. "He's gonna be sorry he ever suggested it."

Sure enough, Harkin was at Tillie's beck and call when she reappeared in his life. "Hey, sweet lady," he bragged in a cavalier way, "I'm willin' t' bury the hatchet. Big deal, so you made a li'l boo-boo that night I took you t' the *Ace in the Hole*."

Tillie acted so syrupy, it was almost sickening. "Gosh, lover" she squeaked, "you're dreamy. I always had this huge crush on ya and am tickled pink t' let bygones be bygones." Ramping up the charm even further, she asked, "You ain't forgettin' 'bout yer invitation to take me out to the racetrack sometime, are ya?"

Harkin brightened, adjusted his tie and tipped his hat jauntily. "I ain't forgettin', Babe," he replied. "I waited months and months for ya t' get back in contact with me. I guess this mess with Wall Street kind o' put a kibosh on everythin'. In spite of all the bad stuff, the good news is that them ponies are still runnin'. The bettin's been pretty hot, too, and the paramutuel system is payin' off like there's no tomorrow."

"Sounds like my kind o' scene," Tillie exclaimed, smacking her lips. "And I'm dependin' on you t' show me the ropes from start t' finish this time, not like in the casino when ya let me run loose like ya did. You gotta be my teacher, got it?"

Snuggling up to her and running a hand along her hip, he snorted, "I'll do more than just teach ya, baby. I'll be *your* pupil and you can teach *me* a few tricks." She permitted him to cop a quick feel, then pulled away abruptly.

"Business before pleasure, Buddy Boy," she purred. "Give me the lowdown on this paramutuel jazz before ya take me out to the track. I ain't fixin' t' be thrown under the bus again by you because I screw up. I'm a quick study, sweetie. I've proven that time and time again, whether on stage, in the recording studio or here in town where the cameras roll and celluloid dreams are made."

Harkin was taken aback. "Gee, snookums," he said sheepishly, "I didn't know you was so poetic. I ain't gonna throw ya under the bus or anywhere else, for that matter. Put yourself in my capable hands 'n you won't be sorry."

Tillie grinned and asserted to the lover boy, gambling man and underworld businessman with whom she had suddenly been reunited, "I ain't got no intention to be sorry. You can count on it."

In the following days Harkin took her to the Los Angeles Turf Club, the Baldwin Racetrack and the brand-spanking new Santa Anita Park. She placed bets adroitly, cheered on her favorite horses and won a sizeable amount of money for Harkin and his cronies. The greedy mob businessman allowed her to keep a little for herself, thinking he was a nice guy for doing so. Tillie had quite a different opinion.

"Jeesh," she carped, "why d'ya have t' be so damn stingy? I'm workin' my tail off, sniffin' the manure them screwy ponies kick up when they run around, not t' mention dyin' out there in the heat every day for ya, and whadya give me? Friggin' crumbs!"

For Tillie it was all an act. She didn't mind what Harkin did as she calculated all the steps she needed to bring him down. Due to her beauty and plucky attitude, she was gaining quite a bit of attention at the track. In addition to being a quick study in the art of knowledge of racing forms, comparing odds and even getting acquainted with some of the owners and trainers of fine thoroughbreds, she made friends easily and developed camaraderie with regulars at Santa Anita. They often relied on her for inside tips and her advice about when and how much to wager.

Harkin took her aside one day to explain something very crucial which was in the process of occurring. "There's scuttlebutt goin' on out there 'bout a horse named Lancelot's Pride. My boys've been keepin' an eye on the trainer and jockey, 'n that pony's been performin' real well. He's been in only a few smaller races 'n things turned out satisfactory. Now they wanna move him up into the higher ranks at Santa Anita, competing against more experienced thoroughbreds. Right now Lancelot's Pride is a longshot, and we've got the inside track on all the bids that've been made so far. They playin' this one strictly behind closed doors, not out at the paramutuel windows. Some big boys in the syndicate have put up some huge piles o' cash on the sly so that the odds stay high. Just between you and me, Tillie, I've got a shitload of money ridin' on this deal, too. If I win this one, you and me ain't gonna have t' worry about a thing, Depression or no Depression."

Blinking, Tillie asked innocently, "Share with you, lover? Don't ya wanna see me put my own money on Lancelot's Pride and win on my li'l ol' lonesome?"

Harkin put his foot down. "No, Tillie," he shouted,

"this time ya gotta lay off. Nobody --- I repeat --- *nobody* goes to the track on this one. All bets are being taken in secret and we're gonna cash in big time when that horsey crosses the finish line in the third race. Too many o' them damn swells know you out there, ya dumb broad."

Reaching for his wallet, he drew out a fresh hundred-dollar bill and thrust it at her. "Take yerself on a shoppin' spree this afternoon. That'll keep yer ass away from the track for the day. Jus' think how you'll be helpin' all them dumbells who're strugglin' out there at their miserable little jobs. Ain't nothin' too good for this screwed-up economy."

Tillie pursed her lips and squealed with delight. "Oh, goodie-goodie-goodie," she gushed. "I'll go to Marcel's o' Beverly Hills and have 'im design me some new frocks. I simply adore lookin' glamorous for my man, y'know." She stroked Harkin's cheek and he smiled generously.

"Marcel o' Beverly Hills, eh?" he remarked. "Yeah, I approve o' that. He's as queer as a three-dollar bill. I don't have t' worry 'bout that fairy pawin' ya like some of th' gorillas in this town. Get goin' already." He patted her on the behind and gave her left butt cheek a little slap.

"Gee, ain't you the romantic one," she said sarcastically. "See ya later, alligator!"

Everything was going according to plan: *Tillie's* plan, that is. Placing the hundred dollar bill in her purse, she ordered a taxi to take her directly to Santa

Anita, defying Harkin's admonitions. She beat a path to the betting windows, intentionally pushing people out of her way so that they would take notice of her prior to the third race.

"Hey," one lanky regular commented discreetly to his companion, a cigar-chomping fat man who clutched his racing form as if he were holding a valuable document, "that's Tillie, Harkin's tomato. She's in a rush to get to the window before the third race."

"Yeah," the cigar-chomper replied, "I noticed. She practically knocked me off my feet when she rushed by. I wonder what the big hurry is. Let's take a gander and see which horse she's placing a bet on."

They needn't have bothered straining to watch, for she made no bones about letting everyone far and wide by the tone of her voice know which horse she favored in the third race. "A hundred on Lancelot's Pride," she yelled, sliding the fresh banknote across to the clerk who hesitated handing her the appropriate ticket.

"The odds are two hundred to one on that nag," the clerk sneered. "You sure you know what you're doing, Lady?"

"Never more sure in my life, Bub" Tillie shot back, grabbing the ticket and disappearing in one of the tunnels leading back to the seating area. Murmurs went through the crowd who had seen and heard her, and fifty or more eager individuals rushed to the windows to place horrendously high bets.

In the next few minutes prior to the third race, the original two hundred to one odds decreased to ninety-five to one. The cigar-chomper fished in his pocket for a nickel and squeezed into a phone booth to call his bookie. Within seconds, word spread about Tillie's appearance at the track and the unusually generous bet she'd placed on a longshot horse. Odds plummeted like stockholders' shares had shattered on Black Tuesday in October of '29. Word soon reached Tom Harkin and he was fuming.

"All the way from two hundred to one down to three to one?" he yelled at his cronies. "How the hell did that happen? If I ever find the rat who double-crossed me on this one, I'll crucify the dirty dealer. I swear, you can't trust anybody in this crooked business!" It sounded amusing, coming from a crook himself.

Tillie had always prided herself in being somewhat of an accomplished escape artist. On a whim she had taken off on Slim Jim, slipped through the prying arms of Frank Cordova and had every intention of dumping Robert Wiseman. Blowing off a nasty customer like Tom Harkin might have required a bit more effort and certainly some caution. After all, he could very possibly hunt her down and put a bullet in her pretty little head.

As she headed toward Baldwin station in a fast moving cab, she formed a mental picture of some of Harkin's goons stalking every port of entry and exit throughout Southern California to prevent her from leaving Los Angeles. She was taking an enormous risk, but with a one-way ticket on the Union Pacific express via the southern route to New Orleans and then onto Miami in her left hand and the key to a locker at the station where she had stored a large suitcase stuffed with travelling essentials in her right hand, her flight from danger was eased to a great degree.

Disguising herself in a shaggy brunette wig and slipping off her elegant frock to reveal underneath a tattered old blouse and a wool skirt which looked worse for the wear also helped her to avoid running into anyone familiar. Wiping her makeup off in the station's lavatory, she glanced in the mirror and barely recognized the person staring back at her. She would travel this way in a second class sleeper all the way to the southernmost tip of Florida.

It would be an understatement to say that Tom Harkin was hopping mad. He and his cohorts were so convinced they could make a real killing on this rigged bet that they sunk their entire bankrolls into the venture. Harkin was only small potatoes in the eyes of the bigshots in the syndicate. Those powerful, influential men acted with much more sophistication than a two-bit hood like him. They treated him like an errand boy and, in some ways, he resented them.

Now he would have to answer to them for the botched plan concerning Lancelot's Pride. He had conceived and nurtured it, assuming total responsibility. He had convinced himself and them that it was foolproof and set them up beautifully. Now it was all bust and he had no idea what the hell had happened.

Fortunately Tillie had covered her tracks so well that Harkin never suspected her involvement for a moment. Instead he directed all his anger at Robert Wiseman, the hapless studio mogul who was practically losing his own shirt due to tremendous financial losses. One of his last big investments had been putting up money for the Baldwin Racetrack. Through bad management he had lost most of the money he put in when fortunes shifted and the site of the new, bigger track was planned for Santa Anita.

It was an honest mistake on Wiseman's part, devastating at best. In Harkin's way of thinking, however, it smelled of betrayal to him and his syndicate cronies. Now was the time to shore up accounts and get even. He had no time to lose. Jumping into his sedan car, he sailed through Arcadia, Sierra Madre, Pasadena and down through the pass leading back to Los Angeles and the tony suburbs of Hollywood. He might well have broken all speed records for auto travel in reaching Wiseman's mansion located above Beachwood Drive.

Chuckling to himself, he reflected, "It's lucky for me I've paid off all these clods workin' for LAPD, otherwise I woulda landed myself a big fat speedin' ticket." He laughed out loud, then refocused his attention on the mission at hand: taking out Robert Wiseman. "That slob's gonna wish he'd never been born on God's green Earth," he added in thought as he raced up the long drive to the mansion.

The grounds which formerly impressed visitors with the neatly trimmed trees and shrubs looked unkempt. There was no one to greet Harkin at the door of the mansion, for the butler, maids, gardener and others servants had long been dismissed. The entire atmosphere reeked of neglect and a certain melancholy. An unsophisticated mobster like Tom Harkin would have not normally noticed such things, but they were too glaring to ignore.

Without knocking he burst through the front door and walked briskly through the foyer to the huge living room. The first thing which struck him was the lack of furnishings. He hunted high and low for Wiseman, finding him at last at the far end of the garden, sitting alone in a beat-up chaise longue and looking extremely forlorn. Harkin brandished a revolver and placed it against the hunched-over man's neck.

"Don't move a muscle, ya rat!" he barked. "I'll shoot yer brains out sooner than look at yer ugly mug." He motioned for the stunned man to get up and walk back into the house with him. "We're gonna open that wall safe o' yours and clean out the cash. You owe me big time, ya louse. I ain't foolin' neither. You gotta debt t' pay and I've come t' collect."

Wiseman stared at him blankly, then burst out laughing. Harkin was taken aback, thinking the man totally insane for behaving so erratically. Didn't the guy know a gun was stuck in his neck, ready for the trigger to be pulled at a moment's notice?

"Th-th-there's n-n-nothing l-l-left," he stuttered. "A-a-all g-g-gone. P-p-poof!" His face took on a vacant look once again. Harkin couldn't make heads or tails of the situation.

"Whadya mean, ya dumb cluck?" he snarled. "How d'ya get t' this point in yer life, after havin' the world by the tail? And makin' all yer money honestly, to boot. I'm a filthy conman, but you, Wiseman? Ya always played it straight 'n narrow."

Wiseman smiled thinly. "Lost," he lamented, having caught his breath and speaking coherently. "One bad investment after another. I know you want to blow me away because of the Baldwin Racetrack fiasco. Believe you me, that was only the tip of the iceberg. It's so bad that they're repossessing everything I own and foreclosing on this place. I'm going to move out to the beach and spend the rest of my days fishing and bumming around." Grinning even more and showing two rows of beautiful teeth, he added, "You wouldn't want to join me, would you, Harkin?"

Harkin dropped his weapon and patted Wiseman on the shoulder. "Nuh-uh," he responded quietly, "you go ahead. Don't mind me. The ocean can wait." Rubbing his chin, he added, "Hey, by the way, look on the bright side, ya sad sack. You ain't lost everythin'. Ya still got yerself that dame Tillie. She ain't chopped liver, y'know."

Wiseman turned to look at Harkin with a mixture of hate and anguish. "Tillie?" he asked incredulously. "Ha! I lost her long ago, you big lug. She ran out on me the moment she had a flicker of success. I understand it's happened frequently in her past, too: Tillie grabs a little bit of fame for herself and leaves bridges burning in the wake. She's a user, pure and simple. Beautiful but dangerous." He hung his head in dismay. "Extremely dangerous. Now, can you do me a big favor and get your ass out of here?"

Harkin obeyed, totally against his usual character of playing the tough guy. The remarks about Tillie haunted him long after he drove back from the Hollywood Hills to his own crib at the edge of Echo Park: a cheap hotel with a flea-bitten mattress and cockroaches scurrying back and forth on the floor and walls. He had hoped to move out of this dump with the winnings from the rigged bet, but it was not to be.

Throwing himself on the bed, he lit a cigarette and stared at the ceiling lamp, a bare lightbulb dangling on a string. He watched smoke drift up as the light flickered. In his jumbled thoughts he drew comparisons between his and Wiseman's similar situations of being down-and-out. Snuffing out the cig and turning his head on the dirty pillow, he mumbled, "Damn that Tillie."

ALEJANDRO VALDEZ'S TRIUMPH

A warm breeze filled the night in Old Havana. Everyone enjoyed a vibrant social life. Walking up and down the *Malecón* and strolling in the promenades near Plaza Vieja, Paseo del Prado and Plaza de Armas, passersby were lured by the flower-sellers and street merchants as they hawked their various wares. Most of these hardworking souls were very poor indeed. It was on an evening like this that the music of my orchestra was most welcome.

I was featured every night at the *Club Rumba de la Habana*, located in the heart of Miramar. And, as usual, the night was sold out. I launched my musicians into several lively dance numbers to delight the enthusiastic audience. People filled the dance floor, grinding to the beat of the rumba, mambo and cha-cha-cha with abandon. I glanced over at a table in the far corner of the salon where a lovely lady sat by herself. Looking her over from top to bottom in the near darkness due to the shadows thrown by the huge columns of the interior of the old building, it suddenly dawned on me who I was devouring with my eyes.

"¡*Ay ay ay*! ¿*Puede ser ella*? Sí, *es mi querida y hermosísima Tillie.*"

When the band had concluded a rousing rendition of *Siboney*, I walked briskly over to her table and embraced her warmly. "Hello, beautiful lady Tillie Thompson!" I cried. "You look wonderful this evening. I hate to be blunt, but what the hell are you doing here?"

Batting her eyelashes in a familiar way, she cooed, "I'll fill ya in later, my Havana Lover Boy."

"I can't tell you what a pleasure it is to see you, my dear. Welcome to Cuba! When we gear up to play again, I'll have the band perform a special dance number, dedicated solely to you, *querida*." We chatted amicably for a bit, then it was time to us resume playing.

I motioned for Tillie to come forward as I introduced her to the crowd during the dedication of the first number for the second set, but she held back.

"Oh, come on, Tillie," I begged, "don't be shy. Do me this favor. Come and have a dance with your Hot Havana Lover Boy!" The crowd egged her on and she could resist no longer since the atmosphere was so charged with excitement. I took her hand gently and brought her to the dance floor as the other patrons cleared away. We danced the first number, then another and another after that until the band had played ten numbers without my direction. Those boys were so talented and really didn't need me. Besides, I was having too much fun with Tillie to leave off. She danced all of the Cuban dances expertly, and regular patrons of the club often applauded and threw compliments and well wishes her way.

I was thrilled to see Tillie again. She seemed more

carefree than ever I remembered her. The band wound up our performance for the club's patrons, and I offered to take Tillie out on the town for the rest of the evening.

"Come with me," I said, "let me show you the wilder side of my beloved Havana."

Tillie blushed. "Goodness me, Alex dear," she murmured, using the English equivalent of my name, "you sure are a romantic devil, ain't ya?"

I made sure Tillie was in good hands. "Only a real Cuban can show you the sights as they've never been seen before. Would you like to take a horse and carriage ride with me? We can start by touring along the *Malecón*. The waves crash against the seawall with even more vigor at night."

Tillie was mesmerized by the sights, sounds, aromas and electrically charged atmosphere of the Cuban capital. "What a swingin' place," she thought. "Ain't got nothin' like this back stateside. And free flowin' booze to boot!" After so much riding and walking, we took a break at Coppelia which was still open and enjoyed our dishes of ice cream under the strings of twinkling lights, rivaled only by the starlit sky. Tillie glanced around once we seated ourselves comfortably.

"I notice lots of Yanks here," she remarked. "What do they all do?"

Shrugging, I replied, "Oh, some come here to retire, others just to spend the weekend, playing. They are in pursuit of the good life, as we know it. Of course even as good as it is, it can't hold a candle to your goodness, *querida*."

Tillie looked away in embarrassment. "You're killin' me with kindness, ya big ol' Cuban masher," she quipped. "Do me a favor and don't stop."

After polishing off two cups of ice cream we lingered in Vedado for a while, making our way once again to the coastline. The streets were virtually empty. I slinked my arm around Tillie as we walked and decided to croon a love song or two to her, *a capella*."

"Gee, Alex," she whispered, "you really know how to treat a gal."

"Tillie," I murmured close to her ear, "I'd consider it a great honor if you'd accompany me to my home this minute." It was apparent that I needn't have coaxed her too much, for her bright smile was all the answer I needed. "Never in my life have I been in the presence of such a lovely creature as you. You captivate me and leave me breathless, my sweet."

Tillie grinned. "You got that right, Mister," she responded. "There's plenty of sweet stuff in me to satisfy your hunger. Take a taste and you'll be beggin' for more, guaranteed."

We reached my oceanfront house in no time. Tillie was visibly impressed with the layout.

"Quite a spread ya got, Alex," she exclaimed. "Simply divine."

"Not as divine as you, Tillie," I said. I went to the bar and poured two small glasses of rum. "Care to join me? I don't know if you've tasted our Bacardi before. It can pack a wallop if you're not used to it."

"Not as much of a wallop you're gonna take when I rumba with ya on that bed ya got in there," she answered, pointing in the direction of my bedroom. That's the moment when I knew that Tillie and I were more than just passing acquaintances. I raised my glass in a toast to her.

"Here's to the sweetest American ever," I proclaimed. "To you, Tillie. May you have long life and even longer love." We dispensed with our rum drinking quickly and were soon thrashing around atop my mattress. Tillie was visibly impressed.

"My blood's boilin', you hot Cuban man," she squealed, "and you're settin' me on fire." The moon and stars shining in the sky visible from my patio enhanced the entire scene.

"Oh, Tillie," I cried, "you are wonderful. Simply marvelous."

"I heard tell Cuba is famous for its sugar cane," she moaned sensually, "but I never imagined I'd find so much sweetness right here between the sheets with you, Big Boy."

The evening in bed with Tillie was the equivalent of witnessing a fireworks show. Rockets sailed into the sky as we both reached our climaxes. Dawn came early in Havana. I cheerfully made breakfast for us, and we downed several cups of strong Cuban coffee with plenty of sugar. Tillie fascinated me with her gorgeous presence.

"You haven't really explained to me what brought you here, Tillie. I know I once invited you when we were both back in Hollywood, but in my wildest dreams I never thought you'd take me up on it."

Sipping her third cup of coffee and nibbling on some toast, Tillie mumbled, "It's a long story, Alex, and I don't wanna bore you t' death with it."

"I'm all ears, my pretty flower," I shot back. "Tell me now, and I won't ask again."

I found out all about her involvement in the entertainment world. "I started out as a dancing girl, dearie. As time went on and my experience grew, I branched out and sang in nightclubs, especially in speakeasy joints where the booze flowed. Y'know, jazz joints, the kind o' places where horny guys would try to grab my tomatoes. I always told 'em to keep their hands away from the merchandise. 'They ain't ripe enough fer ya,' I'd tell 'em, 'so's ya better keep yer dirty hands off.'"

I grinned as Tillie went into all her amusing details, but I didn't laugh outright, of course. "I can see why the men were tempted, Tillie. Your 'tomatoes,' as you say, look ready-freddy to me."

"Ya got one rumba-bumba mind there, Bub," she retorted. "One track, if ya ask me. But it's OK. Anyhow, I graduated to bigger and better stage shows later, performin' in front o' thousands o' suckers. The promoters made thousands o' bucks off me 'cause I was a smash. That led to a recordin' contract. I made me a few shellac sides, y'know."

I simply had no idea how accomplished Tillie was. "A lady of many talents," I exclaimed.

"Oh, I dunno 'bout that. I got bored with it real fast, decided to blow New York and ended up tryin' out for motion pictures out on the Coast. That's where I met you, Louis and the other boys when we were shootin' the vamp movie, remember?"

Tillie finished her coffee and I lighted a cigarette for her. Taking a puff, she continued. "It's funny. The studio head went bust, last I heard of 'im. He made a few more flops after the Marie Antoinette fiasco and ended up broke and a nervous wreck. That kind o' signaled to me t' get outta the picture business, too. After all, I ain't no spring chicken anymore myself."

Shaking my head in protest, I said, "Not at all, Tillie my sweet. You are in your prime, my dear."

She smiled sweetly. "Keep talkin', you slick one. I'll be yours forever if ya don't stop. When you talk in that wacky tropical way you do, my whole body tingles. I'm ready t' follow ya anyway, lover."

Concurring, I replied, "I have never met a woman hotter than you, Tillie, not even here in Cuba which is famous for its hot-blooded *mujeres*."

We sat staring at one another for quite a while. Eventually we ended up on my bed again, thrashing around like rabbits. An idea struck me like a lightning bolt.

"You know, Tillie," I proposed, "even someone as famous as you who slips into the background as you get older always makes a comeback or two, just for old time sake. How would you like to do a so-called farewell performance at our club? The public would love to see you for one last time."

Tillie warmed to the idea. "Sort o' like a last hurrah, huh? Sure, I'm game. Just tell me what I gotta do, snookie ookums."

We spent the next few weeks going over a couple of numbers and rehearsing a routine. Everything we did seemed to thrill her. "Alex," she said breathlessly, "this is like a dream come true, toppin' off my career with this appearance here in Havana." In her usual style, with chest out and strutting confidently, she added, "I'll knock 'em dead here, too. Your Cuban countrymen'll be like putty in my hands."

"Tillie,' I said cautiously, "if you thrust those boobs of yours out anymore, every man in Havana will go crazy for you." I reached for one myself, relishing its firmness. She yielded willingly.

"I reserved that left one especially for you alone, sweetie," she said, laughing seductively. "Others can grab, but only you make my damn nipples stand at attention."

I stood with my hand playfully in a visor position on my forehead. "I salute them, my sweet commander," I quipped, "and am ready to follow your orders, whatever they may be."

The band and I agreed that Tillie's performance should take place on a Saturday evening, since that was always the most crowded night at the club. The manager prepared all the publicity for her appearance, putting up signs everywhere with *"Actuación especial: La Flor de la Primavera Norteamericana Tillie Thompson."* Tillie spent hours with the wardrobe and makeup specialist, preparing herself to perfection. The house was packed as the evening wore on, and the crowd was eager with anticipation. I stepped onto the stage and struck up the band for a few lively numbers to warm things up.

Turning to the audience after the fifth dance song, I grabbed the microphone and took a deep breath for the pivotal announcement. "I'm so grateful to all of you, my fellow citizens of Havana and beyond, for coming out tonight to support our wonderful club. Our special guest is a killer performer. You may know here from her singing, dancing, recording and motion picture career. Now she has come southward to further the cause of Cuban relations with our generous neighbors to the North. Without further ado, here's Tillie!"

The spotlight played upon a tiny but impressive figure in an elegant white evening dress with bright sequins which refracted every bit of sparkle. Her first number was the English language version of *Bésame Mucho*:

Kiss me now,
kiss me with passion —
kiss me as if this were to be
our very last night.
Kiss me now,

kiss me with passion —
for you I may never-more see
once past early light.

She put her entire heart and soul into the song, and rarely had such a lovely, moving version been heard. Tillie was a magnet, electrifying to the point of the audience eating out of her hand. She took several bows and launched into another familiar number, again in English but unmistakable in its intensity: *Quizás quizás quizás*:

You won't admit you love me
And so
How am I ever
To know ---
You only tell me
Perhaps, perhaps, perhaps

Between the two of us we alternated lyrics between Spanish and English, crooning explicitly to one another. We were like two peas in a pod, or to use a slightly more Cuban metaphor, like sugar in the cane. The crowd went wild and shouts of "More, more!" went up all over the huge salon. The scene was perfectly set for a special surprise I had in store, and this was the moment of revelation.

"Ladies and Gentlemen," I announced, "may I have your attention, please. There are times when unexpected events happen in our lives. Having Tillie with me here is one of those events. And I have a special surprise for you, Tillie, one that you could not have possibly guessed."

Reaching into a pocket of my coat, I signaled for a drum roll to heighten the excitement and tension of the moment. A small box containing a sapphire ring was placed between my fingers. I went down on one knee and looked up at Tillie.

"Tillie, my sweetest flower of all," I said loud enough for everyone in the hushed crowd to hear, "would you do me the honor of becoming my wife?"

I could tell that she was pleased and confused at the same time. "Wow, Alex," she cried, "I've heard of love at first sight, and asking for someone's hand shortly thereafter, but in front of all these people? I thought I was gonna have a calf right here on stage!"

The patrons laughed good-naturedly, applauded wildly and prolonged as I slipped the ring on her finger, stood up and embraced her tenderly, kissing her nonstop. "Hey, ya big showoff," she said at one point when we came up for air, "ya didn't ever let me answer. Of course I'll be yer wife, ya big Cuban hunk." Cheers sailed up, almost piercing the smoke-filled room. Glasses were clinked in celebration and shouts of "¡Viva!" and "Long Life!" were heard from many corners of the salon.

"Let's all salute my bride-to-be," I proclaimed at one point amid the noise, "Mrs. Tillie Thompson-Valdez! We''ll rumba the night away."

Tillie looked deeply into my eyes. "Ya got a thing

'bout that rumba, don'tcha. Alex?" she asked. "Sure, I'll do with rumba or whatever dance ya want, forever more.

From that night onward Tillie never left my side. We discreetly celebrated our marriage in a private ceremony and settled down in Miramar as husband and wife. Her desire for attention drove her to ask me on occasion to return for a night or two at the club, belting out a few songs for an appreciative crowd.

All the publicity for those guest appearances featured her name as "Tillie Valdez" each time. She delighted me one night with a poem she'd made up:

Tillie no more shall roam
She made Cuba at last
her home.

If you enjoyed this book, you might also like:

Available in paperback and Kindle formats

at

http://www.amazon.com

and all Amazon sites worldwide

Simply search "ESMERALDA LINTNER"